SYSTEMA PARADOXA

ACCOUNTS OF CRYPTOZOOLOGICAL IMPORT

VOLUME 03

BREAKING THE CODE

A TALE OF THE SKINWALKER

AS ACCOUNTED BY DAVID LEE SUMMERS

NEOPARADOXA

Pennsville, NJ

2021

PUBLISHED BY
NeoParadoxa
A division of eSpec Books
PO Box 242
Pennsville, NJ 08070
www.especbooks.com

ISBN: 978-1-949691-63-4
ISBN (ebook): 978-1-949691-62-7

Interior Design: Danielle McPhail
Cover Art: Jason Whitley
Cover Design: Mike and Danielle McPhail, McP Digital Graphics
Interior Illustration: Jason Whitley
Copyediting: Greg Schauer

DEDICATION

To RODNEY KING
whose stories of life in Gallup, New Mexico
started me on this journey.

Historical Note

In 1942, the town of Gallup, New Mexico actively resisted Executive Order 9066 authorizing the internment of Japanese-Americans during World War II despite its proximity to the major ammunition depot at Fort Wingate. Although not part of the town's official record, this resistance has been reported in numerous newspapers around the United States. This account is fiction, but it is inspired by this notable occurrence.

CHAPTER ONE

Friday, February 20, 1942

Cheryl Davis parked her Ford Coup in the Gallup High School parking lot and walked to the gym under leaden skies. 1942 was off to a dismal start. The United States had declared war against Japan and Germany and now they needed young men to fight their battles for them. As a teacher, she'd been asked to spread the word among former students who might want to enlist in the Marine Corps. The Marine recruiter who contacted her was himself a former student. He showed a special interest in recruiting Navajos well-versed in their native language. Cheryl was part Navajo, on her mother's side, but most wouldn't know it to look at her. She had inherited her strawberry-blonde hair, blue eyes, and fair skin from her father's side of the family.

Cheryl entered the gym and found the bleachers full. The high school band played "The Stars and Stripes Forever." She groaned as a tuba went flat for two notes, but no one else seemed to notice. The crowd cheered and whooped as the band finished the song.

The principal, Sherman Smith, stepped up to the mic. After a burst of feedback, he introduced Cheryl's former student, Duke Ogawa. She smiled as the young man approached the mic. She had taught him during her first year at Gallup High. He'd graduated five years ago. Now he wore a smart blue uniform with yellow and red sergeant's stripes.

"It's good to be back home," Duke said. "I spent a lot of time in this gym learning teamwork and sportsmanship. I'm here today because I need people on my team for something far more important than beating Farmington in the basketball championships." A cheer went up at that and Duke flashed a charming smile. "As you know, the United States is now at war and Uncle Sam needs your Tiger pride and your Tiger courage to defeat the Japanese and the Germans."

"So why does the Marine Corps send a Japanese man to recruit Diné to do their dirty work?" A hush fell over the crowd and all eyes turned to a teacher named Frances Todachine. Cheryl noted the woman used the name the Navajos used for themselves. It was shorthand for the story of how five-fingered people came into the world. The small, wiry Navajo woman had earned a grudging respect around the school because she worked with known troublemakers and helped them find jobs around town when they graduated. Murmurs spread throughout the auditorium. Miss Todachine's words seemed to have struck a chord with the audience.

Duke's smile didn't falter. He waited for the murmuring to die down, then responded with the certainty that had always served him well on the school's debate team. "Ma'am, my parents were born in Los Angeles and moved to Gallup during the last big war to open a feed store. Their action helped feed the troops. The United States is the only country I've known. It's my country."

Cheryl clapped her hands at the succinct, polite response. Soon other people around the gym joined in. An icy chill went down her spine and she glanced toward Miss Todachine. The woman glared at her for a moment, then turned her attention back to Duke.

"Why should Navajos give their lives for a country that killed so many of them?" Miss Todachine shouted so she could be heard over the applause.

The applause ceased and the murmurs resumed.

Another Marine joined Duke at the mic. Cheryl didn't recognize him. "My name is Sergeant Randall Yazzie. My people live over in Arizona, near Show Low." A hush fell over the crowd. The man wasn't a local like Duke, but he was Diné like many people in the audience. "I joined the United States Marine Corps because it gave me the chance to fight for my homeland. Adolf Hitler and Emperor Hirohito want to take our country away from us and we can keep that from happening."

Miss Todachine scowled but fell silent. She couldn't be more than a year or two older than Cheryl, but she carried herself like a much older woman. Several young Navajos huddled with the history teacher and spoke in hushed tones while Duke and Randall continued their presentation. The recruiters highlighted the rewards a soldier could expect, including good pay, regular meals, a pension, and lifetime medical coverage. Cheryl knew these things would all sound good to families who had scraped by through the Great Depression. Although Western New Mexico had been spared the dust storms that plagued the eastern part of the state, Navajos had still suffered through a bad drought.

"You'll get valuable training in the Marines that will help you find a good job after the war," Duke said.

Duke and Randall wrapped up their presentation and mentioned they would go to the gym's foyer and sign up anyone who wanted to enlist. "We'll be back on Monday to make another presentation," Randall said. "Be sure to tell your friends. We're interested in any recruits between the ages of eighteen and forty-four. A bus will pick up those who enlist a week from Monday. It'll take you to Fort Wingate to be sworn in and then we'll catch the train to San Diego where you'll enter boot camp."

They opened the floor to questions. Cheryl feared that Miss Todachine would try to cause more trouble. She couldn't quite understand her fellow teacher's objections. She knew relations between the Navajo—all American Indians, really—and the United States had been strained by westward expansion. She understood the bitterness, but did Miss Todachine really believe that Hitler or Hirohito would be better leaders than Franklin Delano Roosevelt?

Once the question-and-answer session finished, people filed out of the gymnasium into the foyer. Duke and Randall sat at their table and walked a handful of young men through the enlistment process. Cheryl hung back, hoping to speak to Duke. One of her current students, Jerry Begay, approached the recruiters. She couldn't hear what they said to each other, but they shook hands and Jerry signed a piece of paper.

She looked around and noticed Frances Todachine along with a half dozen Navajos standing in the shadows. They also seemed interested in Jerry Begay's conversation with the recruiters. His family had a hogan a short distance from town where they raised sheep. They may be poor, but Jerry's grandmother was a respected matriarch in the Rock Gap clan and he was a good, well-liked student. People paid attention to Jerry and expected him to go far.

As Jerry Begay stepped away from the table, Miss Todachine and her followers seemed to lose interest. They stalked off into the cold night.

That was odd. Miss Todachine wore a fur coat—a strange choice for a Navajo. Most Diné considered wearing a predator's pelt taboo. Then again, Cheryl couldn't see the coat well in the dim lighting. It could well have been rabbit or imitation fur. Even with her fair skin, Cheryl wouldn't wear fur at a gathering with so many Diné. There could be talk that the person wearing the fur might practice witchcraft. Though Cheryl was only part Navajo, she had grown up here. She knew the legend of the skinwalkers, witches who sought the knowledge of magic for power, not healing. Whether she believed or not, she would never give the community a reason to wonder about her the way Miss Todachine did.

Cheryl made a point of stopping Jerry Begay on his way out. "Did you just sign up?"

He flashed her a broad smile. "Yes, ma'am."

"I'm pleased you want to defend your country, but don't you think it would be a good idea to finish your high school diploma first?"

He shrugged. "I'm eighteen. I don't need my diploma to enlist. What I'll get from the Marines is more than the diploma will be worth. Plus, they said I'd get extra pay because I speak Navajo."

Cheryl narrowed her gaze. "Did they say why that would give you extra pay?"

Jerry shook his head. "I should get going, my parents want me home before it gets too late."

Cheryl sighed and nodded. "Have a good night. Will I see you in class on Monday?"

He nodded. "I'll be there. The bus won't come through for new recruits for another week."

"Good."

As Jerry left the gym, Cheryl began to wonder if Miss Todachine was right to question these recruiters.

"Penny for your thoughts?"

Duke Ogawa's voice made her jump. He no longer sat behind the recruiting table, but had come up behind her.

"Sorry, didn't mean to startle you, Miss Davis."

Cheryl put her hand to her chest and smiled. "It's good to see you, Duke. It looks like the Corps is treating you well."

He nodded and smiled. "Actually, my enlistment ended last month, but I signed on again after Pearl Harbor."

Cheryl sighed. "Yeah, it's a bad business and I'm glad the United States is finally taking a stand against the fascists and the imperialists, but..." Her voice trailed off as she followed the direction Jerry had gone.

"You don't like seeing kids as young as Jerry Begay signing up for war," he guessed.

She nodded.

Duke led Cheryl back to the table and introduced his partner. "Randall Yazzie, this is Miss Cheryl Davis, she was my math teacher here my senior year."

"Pleased to meet you, ma'am" Yazzie said. "Call me Rand. So, who was that woman with the smart mouth?"

"Oh, that's Frances Todachine." Cheryl shrugged. "She's a history teacher. She actually does good work with a lot of the kids. She helps them find jobs."

"I got a strange feeling from her." Rand shook his head. "I can't quite put my finger on it, but there was something more than concern going on there."

"Yeah, she had a chip on her shoulder. She was looking for a fight," Duke said.

"Single woman, a group of close followers, all men," Rand mused. "Back home, there'd be talk…"

Cheryl snorted a laugh. "You don't think she's having an affair with any of those young men, do you?"

Rand shook his head. "That wouldn't be the worst of it." He leaned in close and whispered. "They'd be talking witchcraft."

As Jerry Begay drove home from the recruitment rally at the high school, snow began to fall. At first just a few light flurries drifted through the air, then the flakes fell heavier as he cleared the city limits and drove the ten miles south to his family's land. Smoke wafting from the stovepipe poking from his family hogan's roof gratified him. It would be warm inside. His mother no doubt left some stew on the fire for him. He guessed two inches of snow already blanketed the ground by the time he walked from the pickup to his front door.

The hogan was a small, cozy home. A cast-iron wood stove sat in the building's center and the scents of lamb and vegetables simmering told him he had been correct about her having dinner ready for him.

"Yá'át'ééh," his father said, speaking the traditional Diné greeting, which asked whether Jerry was well.

Jerry responded by saying he was well, "yá'ánísht'ééh," and sat down at the table. His mother brought him a bowl of stew and he began to wolf it down.

"So, how was the meeting?" asked Jerry's mother, Maria.

"Good," Jerry said. "Lots of people showed up." He took another bite, then swallowed. "I signed up." He said the last quietly.

Jerry's father, Javier, frowned. "We need you here on the farm this season more than ever."

"You need to finish your high school diploma," his mother chastened.

"I'll earn money faster in the military and I'll get skills that can help me after I'm back." Everything the recruiters had said about joining up sounded better than continuing to feed sheep and take boring old classes. "Besides, if people don't go, evil men like Adolf Hitler will send his soldiers to take our lands away from us."

"It has happened before, and we have survived." His father sounded tired.

"You sound like that history teacher at school, Miss Todachine." Jerry scooped up the last of his stew.

His mother's jaw tightened. "Don't speak her name in this house."

"What?" Jerry shrugged. "She's just a loud-mouthed do-gooder. She found a job for John Claw, of all people. I thought the sheriff would throw him in jail for sure."

Maria Begay nodded. "She consorts with all kinds of trouble-makers and keeps them from finding justice. She spends way too much time with those high-school boys."

Jerry snorted a laugh. "She's not much older than we are. She's gotta spend time with someone." He took his bowl to a washtub near the wood stove and put it in to soak until the morning when it could be washed.

"Mark my words, she's trouble," Maria reiterated. She walked over to the woodstove and tossed in more wood from a nearby stack.

"When would you leave us?" Javier's eyes narrowed.

"A bus will come through Gallup week after next. It'll take us to Fort Wingate where we'll be sworn in, then they'll take us to San Diego for training."

Javier grunted. "California is very far. How long will you be away?"

"Three years," Jerry said.

Maria put her hand to her chest. "So long?"

Jerry held out his hands. "I'll talk to the guys at school. I can find someone to help you here on the farm." He walked over and gathered his mother up into his arms. For the first time he could remember, she looked sad and frail.

"Our need for help is not our main concern," Jerry's father said. "We'll miss you."

Jerry gave his mother a squeeze then sat down opposite his father. "If this were the old days, warriors would be sent out to meet a threat. This is no different."

Javier pursed his lips and nodded. "I suppose you're right…"

"But three years?" His mom shook her head.

"I'll write," Jerry promised. "And if you guys ever let them install a telephone out here, I could probably call now and then."

"We'll consider it," Maria said, "but only for this reason."

Javier reached out and took his son's hand. "We'll miss you, but I understand why you believe this is necessary." He stood and walked over to the bed. "Now, this snow is arguing with my bones. I think it's time to get some sleep."

The hogan didn't allow much room for privacy. Many families had moved into homes in town, only to lose those homes during the Great Depression and return to traditional dwellings out on their land. Jerry's family was one of those. His parents had a bed along one of the hogan's walls. Jerry's bed was along the wall across from it. They'd set up an old-fashioned privacy screen between the two. Jerry's dad blew out the oil lamp next to him. Cloth rustled as Jerry's parents changed into their nightclothes.

Jerry followed suit and climbed under a stack of warm blankets. Despite the snowstorm outside, he was snug in his family's home. The idea of sharing a barracks with other soldiers didn't bother him. His parents began to snore, and the wind whipped outside. His eyes grew heavy and he began to drift off to sleep.

Tap. Tap. Tap.

The tapping caused his eyes to spring open. No trees grew up against the hogan to cause the noise. He listened. Maybe he'd just dreamed the sound as he'd started to drift off to sleep. His parents still snored. Whatever he had heard, it hadn't awakened them. His eyelids grew heavy again.

Tap. Tap. Tap.

Again, Jerry's eyes sprang open. The tapping resumed. It sounded like it came from the wall beside him. He tried to picture the outside of the hogan. He didn't think there was anything there but grass. The wall had been constructed from solid logs. Nothing light could make a tapping loud enough to wake him. He tried to dismiss it as his imagination.

Wide awake now, he thought more about the Marine Corps. He wondered what boot camp would be like. He had no doubt he would cut it. He'd been up early in the morning and working hard ever since his family moved back out to their traditional lands. His chest swelled with pride as he thought about continuing the long tradition of Navajo warriors.

Tap. Tap. Tap.

The sound returned. No doubt about it, this was no dream. He thought more about what could cause the tapping. He wondered if some wood had broken loose in the high winds, or if the roof had been damaged. It could probably wait until morning, but he thought he'd better go check it out. He wouldn't get to sleep until he knew what it was. He shoved back the blankets, pulled on his trousers and heavy boots, and lit the lamp.

As he walked toward the door, he looked back at his parents. Still asleep. He went outside. The snow was coming down heavier than before and swirled in white eddies. He stayed close to the house, so as not to get lost in the storm, crunching through snow deeper than the tops of his boots. He reached the back wall of the octagonal structure, and inspected the building.

There were divots in the snow, as though an animal had been there and left. Had a sheep gotten loose and butted the wall?

He held up the lantern and looked around.

In the distance stood a tall figure on two legs. Its long ears lay back and it snarled, revealing long, sharp teeth. A forbidden word came to mind — a word as shocking as the vilest pornography. Although this did not involve ripping off clothes, it involved ripping off the very skin to reveal the monster underneath.

Yee naaldlooshii in the Diné language.

Skinwalker in English. It didn't mean the same thing, but it sounded almost worse.

The creature turned and walked away.

He knew he should follow his path back to the front door, blow out his lantern, and forgot what he'd seen. Good sense almost prevailed, but curiosity got the better of him. He took a step away from the house and then another.

The skinwalker continued to prowl through the snow.

Jerry followed a few more steps.

The wind picked up. The snow came down faster until he lost sight of the creature.

He ran forward a few more steps, heart pounding furiously. The skinwalker had vanished.

The cold began to seep through his clothes. He needed to get back inside before the storm grew worse. All he had to do was keep a clear head, turn around and follow his path. When he turned, he could no longer see his footprints. He could no longer see the hogan. He should only be a few steps away. He began trudging the direction he thought home should be. Despite the cold, exhaustion came over him. It would be so good to lie down and go to sleep.

Chapter Two

Saturday, February 21, 1942

The scents of bacon and coffee wafted through the house as Sheriff Chuck Davis stood in the bathroom shaving on Saturday morning. He finished up, put on his shirt, and strode to the kitchen where his daughter, Cheryl, cooked breakfast. He had good, strong kids. They'd helped him weather the storm of his wife's passing from cancer a little over a decade ago. Now his son served in the Navy—he said he wanted to get as far away from sand and sagebrush as he could. Cheryl had gone off to New Mexico Normal University to get her teaching certification, then came back. He wondered if she'd caught the eye of any nice young men yet? With so many going off to war, he figured it might be a while before she married.

Cheryl turned around. "Good morning."

"Good morning." Davis leaned over and kissed his daughter's cheek. "Breakfast smells good." He took the percolator off the stove and poured himself a cup of coffee, then walked over to the sink to look outside. The sky had cleared, but it looked like the storm had dumped a good six inches. He hoped he wouldn't have to go out.

He turned to face his daughter. "You seem quiet this morning. Anything the matter?"

She shrugged as she took the last of the bacon from the pan and started frying some eggs. "Just thinking about the recruitment meeting last night."

"Oh, I thought you said it went well. They had lots of kids sign up." Davis sat down at the kitchen table.

"They did. It's Miss Todachine. She raised some objections about Navajos going off to fight in the war." Cheryl flipped the eggs. "I don't agree with her, but I don't think she's wrong to be concerned."

The sheriff shrugged. "That's people for you."

Cheryl transferred the eggs onto plates, placed one at her father's place and one at hers, then sat down. "What bothered me was how ready Duke Ogawa's friend from Show Low was willing to accuse her of practicing witchcraft."

Davis shook his head. "Some people don't like it when women speak up and make their opinions heard. They find ways to dismiss them."

"Do you believe these witch people exist?"

He shrugged. "New Mexico's a funny place. There are court records of people accusing others of witchcraft in the territorial days, not even fifty years ago." He took a bite of his breakfast while he thought. "Sometimes I drive the highways around here and I think I see something strange, like an animal running beside my car even when I'm going faster than any animal can run. When I stop to look, it's gone. I can see how these stories get started."

Before he could say more, the phone rang. He pushed his chair back, but Cheryl held out her hand. "I'll get it." A moment later, she looked at her father with a note of apology. "It's Deputy Hancock. He needs to talk to you."

Davis rose to his feet and took the receiver from his daughter. Deputy Hancock told him Javier Begay came into the station. He found his son dead in the snow at his place down on Highway 602 and suspected murder. The sheriff frowned. "I take it they've plowed down there."

"They got it a little while ago. Otherwise, Begay wouldn't have made it into town to report the crime.

Davis sighed. So much for a quiet day. "All right. Tell him to get back home and I'll be down there as soon as I can. Call the hospital and have them send an ambulance, and you better alert the coroner." The sheriff hung up, returned to the table, and wolfed down the rest of his breakfast. He explained what happened between bites and gulps of coffee.

Cheryl dropped into her chair, stunned. "Jerry's dead? I... I didn't mean..." She struggled to get the words out. "Who would want to kill him?"

Davis shrugged. "No idea. I'll see what I can learn." He went to the bedroom and retrieved his badge, hat, and gun, then returned to the kitchen. He kissed his daughter again and wiped a tear from her cheek. "What do you plan to do?"

"I was planning to work on my ham radio project." She reached for a napkin and blew her nose. "Now I'm not sure I can, given what happened to Jerry."

"Take some time for your hobby. It'll do you good." He stepped to the door. "I'll let you know what I find out."

"Be careful." Cheryl waved at her father.

The snow on the road in front his house had started to melt, but Davis still had to shovel out the driveway—at least enough to get his Mercury Eight patrol car out to the street. When he finished, he turned onto the road and drove down the highway to the Begay place. As he drove, he thought how all the melting snow would make for slick and treacherous roads over the weekend when it froze again that night.

He turned down the dirt drive that led to the Begay's farm. No plow had been through, but Javier Begay must have gone out in his Ford pickup. Davis followed the ruts in the snow to the plot of land with a hogan, an outhouse, and sheep pens. The landscape around looked pristine and white. The only evident footprints were a set around the hogan, and a set to and from the truck. The sheriff trudged to the door and knocked. Javier answered and invited the sheriff inside. Maria Begay sat in a chair, hugging herself, tears running down her cheeks.

"Can you tell me what happened?" Davis asked.

"We woke up this morning and found Jerry's bed empty. I thought he just woke up before us and went to the outhouse. Maria started breakfast. I went out to check on the sheep, make sure they were all right with the sudden cold. That's when I noticed Jerry's body in the snow behind the hogan."

"My deputy said you thought he'd been murdered."

"My boy had good sense. He wouldn't have gone out into the storm on his own. He wouldn't have stayed long enough to have died," Javier said.

"Do you mind showing me where he is?"

Javier caught his breath. "I'd rather not."

Sheriff Davis expected that answer. He'd grown familiar with the Navajo taboo about approaching dead bodies. There were rituals for disposing of the dead so one wouldn't contract ghost sickness. "I asked for an ambulance to meet me here. Do you have any problem with us taking his body back to the hospital so the medical examiner can take a look?"

Javier looked conflicted as his desire for justice battled with tradition. Maria put her hand on her husband's arm but met the sheriff's gaze. "Do what you need to do."

Davis nodded. "I'll go check the crime scene, but I'll talk to you before I leave." He stepped outside and followed the footprints around the hogan. Jerry Begay lay in the snow, partially covered. The sheriff approached and knelt down beside the body. He saw no sign of a gunshot wound or blunt trauma. If someone had approached Jerry, their tracks were obscured by the snow. The sheriff stood and looked around. Something on the house's nearest wall caught his eye. He stepped over and took a closer look. A few hairs jutted out from the wall. They were so light they were almost blonde. They felt coarse, like coyote or dog hair. The color reminded him of a golden retriever, just a few shades darker than Cheryl's hair. There was no telling how long they had been there before.

Hearing a vehicle crunch through the snow, Davis walked back around to the front of the hogan to see the ambulance pulling up. He waved at the driver and his assistant. They unloaded a stretcher and brought it around to the back. As the sheriff helped them load Jerry's body he took another look. Still no sign of a wound — no blood on the ground.

The sheriff looked up at the ambulance driver. "If you had to guess, what killed this young man?"

The driver shrugged. "I'm no expert, Sheriff, but I'd say he died of exposure."

"That's what I'm thinking." He nodded to the men and they carried the body back around to the ambulance. The sheriff walked around the scene twice more before returning to the hogan's front door. He found Javier and Maria standing just outside, watching the ambulance drive away.

"Do you have any idea what time your son went out?"

Javier shook his head. "It was dark, and it was after Maria and I went to bed."

Davis looked around and saw no clocks. He took out a notepad and a pencil.

"Why do you think your son was murdered?"

"He just signed up to join the Marine Corps," Javier said. "Not everyone around here approves of Navajos joining the white man's military."

"I saw no sign he was attacked." Davis shrugged. "It looks like a tragic accident to me."

"There are some who practice dark magic." Javier leaned close and whispered. "Some say that's how Joe Nez north of town acquired so much land. And Jerry told us that Miss Todachine woman was at the meeting last night. I wonder about her, too. One of them could have lured our boy out into the snow."

"Why would one of them drive all the way out here to do that? What would they have to gain?"

"They wouldn't drive. They would use magic to summon the…" Javier seemed to search for the right word. After a moment he leaned forward and whispered. "They would summon the spirit of a skinwalker to themselves and it would give them the power to do this terrible thing."

The sheriff closed his notebook and returned it to his pocket. "I'm sorry, I don't see any evidence of foul play. We'll see what the coroner says and I'll let you know. I'm very sorry for the loss of your son."

Daisuke "Duke" Ogawa entered Fort Wingate's mess hall. Enlisted army men fell silent. He tried to decide if that was because of his Japanese heritage or his Marine Corps uniform. He noticed two guys he'd gone to high school with and waved at them, calling out their names.

"Hey, Duke," one of them called back. When he did, the buzz around the mess hall resumed and Duke was just another NCO in for some chow. He went through the line, grabbed breakfast, and found an empty table.

Fort Wingate was a hive of activity. Even before the United States declared war against the Axis powers, it had been slated to become the primary ordnance depot for the army in the Southwestern United States. Soldiers and civilians swarmed around the base erecting housing, storage facilities, and even locomotive repair shops for the trains coming through to pick up ordnance and take it to the coast. Colonel R.S. Barr had just assumed command of the base and he seemed determined to make Fort Wingate the best ordnance depot in the United States Army.

Rand Yazzie entered the mess hall as Duke sat down. Again, the buzz quieted. Despite his Marine Corps uniform, chatter resumed more quickly this time. Rand went through the chow line and joined Duke at the table. "Pretty good night last night," he said.

Duke shook his head. "Didn't sign up as many as I'd hoped." He looked around the mess hall. He noticed most of the guys in uniform were white. "Navajos don't seem to be signing up in droves."

Rand snorted. "Mostly, that's because they haven't been asked. There are quite a few who work here at the base, they're just not soldiers." He sipped a cup of coffee, then made a face. "I thought the coffee at Camp Pendleton was bad. This stuff is vile."

"It should wake you up, though." Duke smiled.

Rand turned around and looked through the window at the snow on the ground. "Yeah, on days like this, I just want to stay warm under the blankets." He turned around and faced Duke. "Cuddling up with someone pretty would be nice, too. You wanna tell me about that teacher we met last night?"

Duke frowned. "It's nothing like that. She was my math teacher."

Rand laughed. "My math teacher in Show Low didn't look anything like that. He was an old man about two years from retirement. If I'd had your teacher, I would have had a hard time concentrating on my work."

"Well, a few ideas did cross my mind when she made us graph polynomial functions, but she was my teacher. I'm sure she didn't share any of those feelings." Duke shook his head and focused on his breakfast.

"Are you sure?" Rand winked. "She seemed awfully glad to see you last night. Maybe you should give her a call."

Duke looked up and met his partner's eyes. "We're only here for a few days."

"We won't be in the Corps forever and this is your home." Rand shrugged. "What harm would a movie do?"

Duke considered firing back a retort but stopped himself. Rand had a point and Cheryl Davis had always seemed nice. He took a moment to do some mental math and figured she couldn't be much more than five years older than him. Might be a little weird, but not a lot weird. He decided he'd see whether she returned to the high school recruitment rally on Monday night. If so, he'd ask her out for sure.

An army corporal stepped up to Duke and Rand's table. "Are you Yazzie and Ogawa?"

"We are," Rand affirmed.

"Colonel Barr wants to speak with you in his office."

"Thanks, corporal. Can we follow you over?"

The corporal gave them a nod. Duke and Rand took their trays to the cleaning rack, then followed the corporal out of the mess hall and down a shoveled path to the two-story, brick administration building. Upstairs, the corporal knocked on an office door and disappeared inside. He returned a moment later. "The colonel will see you now."

Duke and Rand entered the colonel's office and snapped salutes, which the colonel returned. "Please, be seated."

They sat down and the corporal left.

"I hear you had a good turnout at your recruitment drive, last night," the colonel said.

"We did, sir," Duke affirmed. "We filled the bleachers and a dozen young men signed up."

"We're looking forward to getting over to Grants tonight," Rand said.

"I understand you're especially interested in recruiting Navajos for an experimental program, sending transmissions in their own language." The colonel folded his hands on the desk.

"Yes, sir," Rand said. "There was an experiment done back in 1918 during the Great War where Indians sent signals. The Krauts never broke that code. We hope to do the same thing now but on a larger scale."

The colonel pursed his lips. "The Krauts have had over twenty years to learn how to speak Indian. Are you sure it's going to work again?"

"With all due respect, those Indians were Cherokee and Choctaw," Rand explained. "There's very little written Navajo and it's a whole different language family than they used in 1918."

"Interesting. I hope it works out for you." The colonel sat back. "We have a lot of Navajos working here at the depot. They can be hard workers, but it's not always easy working with them."

Duke looked from the colonel to Rand. He wondered whether the colonel knew that Rand was Navajo... or cared.

"They don't always show up at a set time. You can't get them to sweep buildings. When I took this assignment, I was told Navajos were a matriarchal society. I woulda thought men were used to household chores."

Rand folded his arms and narrowed his gaze, but forced a smile. "I'm afraid it doesn't always work like that, sir. May I make a suggestion?"

"If it'll help, I'm all ears, son."

"Put out the word you want to hire a medicine man to purify the buildings here at the depot. Part of the ritual is sweeping the buildings. The medicine man will be glad for the money and you'll get the sweeping done."

"Very interesting." The colonel gave a slow nod. "I'll give that some thought." He leaned forward again and then looked from Rand to Duke. "That's not why I called you in here, though. I wanted to give you a head's up that I got a call last night from one of the teachers at Gallup High School. She was concerned about having a Japanese soldier at her school recruiting young men to fight overseas."

"Sir, was her name Frances Todachine?" Duke asked.

The colonel pursed his lips and nodded. "I believe it was."

"We're sorry she bothered you, sir. We're not trying to make waves."

"It could be more serious than that." The colonel stood and walked to the window. "Have you boys heard about Executive Order 9066?"

Duke looked to Rand, who seemed as perplexed as he was. "No, sir," Rand said.

"Not surprised," the colonel said. "President Roosevelt signed it on Thursday. You were probably still on the train on the way over here. The order authorizes the secretary of war and any military commanders he designates, the authority to set up consignment zones for people of Japanese descent."

Duke forgot himself and jumped to his feet. "What?"

The colonel didn't bother to point out Duke's breach of protocol. "I've got enough to worry about without figuring out where I'd house the Japanese people of McKinley County. That's not the point. The executive order has some people worked up. If someone accused you of spying or engaging in untoward activity, they might force my hand. I might have to lock you in the stockade until the next train came back through for California." He turned around. "I don't want to do that. Am I understood?"

Duke swallowed and snapped a smart salute. "Understood, sir. I will do everything I can to keep out of trouble."

"Good. Dismissed."

Randall stood up and saluted. In lockstep, the two Marines left the office. Duke's thoughts turned to his family in Gallup. His mouth went dry. He could deal with whatever came his way, but it would break his heart to see them lose everything they'd gained since moving to New Mexico.

Chapter Three

Monday, February 23, 1942

Cheryl noticed when she returned to the high school on Monday evening there were significantly less cars and trucks in the parking lot. She parked her car and walked to the gym. Even out in the foyer, among the trophy cases and photos of games, the crowd seemed quieter and more subdued. When she turned the corner and entered the gym, her suspicions were confirmed. At most, the bleachers were half full. After Friday night's snowstorm the weather had cleared up, but turned bitter cold. Snow on the road had melted just enough to freeze into treacherous sheets of ice. Cheryl knew that kept some people away, but it wasn't the whole story.

She could have chosen a seat anywhere, but she climbed to a point high in the bleachers, so she could get a good view. Scanning the crowd, she saw no sign of Miss Todachine or her followers. During the day at work, the history teacher had strutted through the corridors looking smug and confident. Miss Todachine—Cheryl could never bring herself to think of the woman as Frances—looked at her and grinned. All Cheryl could think of at the time was the Big Bad Wolf from Grimm's Fairy Tales.

Cheryl shuddered at the memory, glad her fellow teacher had decided to skip tonight's proceedings. At the front of the gym, Duke and his partner Randall leaned toward each other, talking while the band played. She waved and was glad to see a smile light Duke's face. He gave a small wave back.

The high school band's performance of "The Stars and Stripes Forever" was better than the one from Friday night, but the cheers at the song's conclusion were more subdued. It wasn't just that there were fewer people in attendance. Those people seemed less excited than on Friday night. News about Jerry Begay's death had spread, damping enthusiasm for local boys to come out and hear the servicemen speak.

Principal Smith came up to the microphone and introduced Randall Yazzie. Cheryl narrowed her gaze. It seemed as though he made a point of omitting Duke. Rand stepped up to the mic and told a story familiar to many of the kids around Gallup. He'd grown up as one of three kids in a hogan outside of Show Low, Arizona. His family raised sheep and kept a small garden. They struggled to make ends meet.

He joined the Marine Corps where the skills he'd learned on the farm served him well. Rising early, growing up strong, taught the ways of a warrior, he had no problem breezing through boot camp. He sounded genuine. Cheryl smiled to herself wondering how much of the story was true and how much was just a line. She knew many young Navajos talked the talk of being warriors, but so many of the old ways had been forgotten. She wondered if Randall had known traditional teachers who truly taught him.

Randall then launched into a description of Adolph Hitler marching across Europe, conquering nation after nation, making them all learn to speak German. Even though he delivered his speech in English, the words would have a particular impact on the Diné in the audience, all of whom heard stories of their parents hauled off to Indian Schools and forced to speak English. This was an experience they didn't want to repeat.

Cheryl noticed no mention of Emperor Hirohito taking his troops through the Pacific as had been done on Friday night. Duke had delivered that part of the presentation. She hoped he felt all right. From where she sat, he looked fine, just a little subdued.

Next, Randall talked about the opportunities to learn a trade. Cheryl thought back to her years of college. Given the choice, she would have studied electronics or physics, but she'd known opportunities for women were rare in those fields. Would she join the military to learn a trade if she could? She thought she might.

As far as she knew, though, the only opportunities for women in the armed services were serving as nurses in medical units, which didn't interest her. Still, she might ask Duke or Rand what other opportunities there were for women. She had learned skills in college, which would allow her to fend for herself in difficult situations.

Randall went on to tell the audience about training at Camp Pendleton. "It'll be the hardest, most grueling time of your lives, but I know you're tough and you can make it. I will let you in on one good thing about training. There's no snow in San Diego this time of year."

That last actually brought cheers and applause.

He concluded his presentation by saying they would sign people up in the foyer after the rally.

Finally, Principal Smith invited everyone to stand for the National Anthem. The band played and Cheryl put her hand over her heart. Once the band finished playing, she worked her way down the bleachers.

In the foyer, kids shuffled by the desks, on their way out the door. She hung back and listened as people murmured. There were whispers about Jerry Begay and how he'd been lured out into the snow. "Deputy Hancock told my dad the sheriff found hairs out their place. You don't suppose it was a…" The person who spoke didn't complete the thought, but she suspected she knew the word he didn't say: skinwalker.

Cheryl turned and approached the desk. Randall rifled through papers on a clipboard and Duke's brow was furrowed.

"What's going on? It seems no one wants to sign up tonight," Randall said.

"Gosh," Cheryl said. "I guess you didn't hear. Jerry died Friday night. He walked out into the snow. My dad investigated. It looked like there were white-out conditions and he lost his way."

One of Cheryl's students tapped her on the shoulder. She followed him a few steps away. He looked from one side to the other as though seeing who might overhear. "Miss, I don't think he just walked out. My dad knows Jerry's dad. Jerry's old man thinks a... skinwalker lured him out into the storm."

Cheryl swallowed and nodded. She tried to speak but words wouldn't come at first. She blew out a deep breath and plunged ahead. "That's terrible. I... hope that's not true."

The young man nodded, then retreated out into the cold. Cheryl returned to the table.

"What was that all about?" Randall asked.

"My student tells me he thinks a skinwalker is responsible for Jerry's death."

Duke stood up beside Randall. "They really are taking this skinwalker thing seriously."

Principal Smith approached and cleared his throat, interrupting the conversation. "I'm sorry we didn't get a better turnout for you tonight. After the enthusiastic response we had on Friday, I was sure people would tell their friends."

Rand smiled. "The roads are icy and it feels like another storm's approaching. It's also Monday night. A lot of people usually just want to stay in."

The principal snorted. "Most young people in a town like Gallup are looking for any excuse to get out." He stepped close. "It's really unfortunate about Jerry Begay's death. I think that spooked a lot of people, even if it had nothing to do with him enlisting."

"Let's give it one more shot, sir," Duke suggested. "We're scheduled to give a presentation in Farmington on Wednesday and we're going to Grants again on Thursday. Friday worked well before. I'd like to try a third presentation on Friday night."

"Friday sounds good. I'm happy for Gallup High School to do its part for the cause." The principal reached out and shook the soldiers' hands, then turned around and left.

Rand sighed. "Another opportunity is good, but unless the rumors about a skinwalker or a witch die down, it could keep them from coming out to hear us."

A hollow spot formed in the pit of Cheryl's stomach. She felt powerless to help reassure the recruiters and she hated it when she felt powerless. "If this is the only incident, the whisperings will eventually die down."

Rand nodded. "I hope so. All I know is that Friday I saw a dozen brave young men willing to stand up for their country. Today, those who are brave enough to be here at all are still looking over their shoulder."

Cheryl flashed an encouraging smile. "I'll talk to my dad. As I said, he's the sheriff. Maybe he knows something that can help quell any rumors." She looked at her watch. "It's getting late. I'd better go." She waved and began to step outside.

Duke hurried around the table. "Let me walk you to your car."

"You don't have to," Cheryl said.

"I want to."

They walked out into the parking lot together.

"I don't know if these are the best circumstances, but I have tomorrow night off." Duke looked down and shuffled his feet. "Would you like to go see a movie?"

Cheryl stifled a grin. She remembered him like this whenever she'd posed an especially difficult math question in class. "I think that would be fun. They're showing that new Lon Chaney film, The Wolf Man downtown tomorrow."

"I didn't think that would be your cup of tea," Duke said.

"There's a lot you don't know about me." She took out a slip of paper, wrote down an address, and handed it to Duke.

"I'll see you tomorrow. When's the early show?"

"Start's at seven."

"Pick you up for dinner at 5:30?"

"That would be delightful."

She grinned and Duke also flashed a smile before returning to the gym. As he walked away, she couldn't bear the thought of something happening to him on the dangerous, icy roads. That feeling of powerlessness returned and knotted her stomach again.

"Don't you look like the cat that ate the canary," Randall said as Duke approached. "I take it she said yes to a movie?"

Duke shrugged. "I have no idea if this will go anywhere. It'll just be nice to get away from the base for a while."

"No doubt she'll be easier on the eyes than looking at those ground pounders over at Fort Wingate."

Rand and Duke gathered up their papers into two cases and took them out to their Willys MB. As they did, a few snow flurries drifted from the sky. "Looks like another wintry night," Duke remarked. He shivered as he looked at the vehicle's canvas top and sides.

"You flatlanders just don't know how to drive in snow. This is nothing compared to the storms we'd get up in the high country around Show Low." Despite his confidence, Rand looked up at the sky, as though worried about how strong the storm would get. He climbed into the vehicle and cranked over the 4-cylinder engine.

They drove through town and soon sped along Route 66 toward Fort Wingate.

"So, what do you think is spooking kids around here and keeping them from signing up?" Duke's gaze drifted outside. Between the clouds and the first quarter moon, he couldn't see much outside the range of the headlights.

Rand shrugged. "You're the local boy, you tell me."

"The only thing I know for sure is the death of the Begay kid, but that sounds like an accident." The headlight beams seemed to catch something in the bushes to the car's right. Duke narrowed his gaze, trying to get a better view of whatever it was.

"If rumors of a skinwalker are going around…" Again, Rand shrugged. "…it could really spook people, keep them away."

"My grandma used to tell us stories about the Yuki-onna, a snow maiden back in Japan who would lure the unwary to their deaths. The idea absolutely terrified me on nights like this until I was about ten years old. After that, I realized it was just a story." Again, Duke thought something moved just outside the headlight beams.

The snow began to fall harder.

"You grew up here, so you know how much we Diné respect our medicine men," Rand said. "They study long years to learn how to help people. Doesn't it make sense that some people also would study just as hard for selfish reasons?"

Duke laughed. "Come on, man, really? A medicine man learning how to change into an animal?"

"I don't know whether a skinwalker literally changes into the animal or if they summon some strange creature from another world, or if they just use their reputation to scare people. No matter what actually happens, it gives the person a kind of power over others." The jeep fishtailed over some ice and Rand slowed down a little.

Duke glanced outside again. This time, he was sure something ran beside them. He pulled down the window flap and shone his flashlight outside. He gasped at the sight. A creature loped alongside them, keeping pace with the vehicle. He wasn't sure what to make of it at first. It was long and spindly like an over-grown jackrabbit. Longish ears helped that impression. Over the years, he'd seen big jackrabbits, but never one this big.

It turned and looked right at him, eyes catching the flashlight beam and glowing green. He then got a better look at the creature's face — a coyote.

Duke yanked the window flap back up.

"How fast are we going?"

Randall checked the speedometer. "Forty miles per hour."

"There's some freaky coyote running right beside us, keeping pace." Duke lowered the flap again. The creature had vanished.

Randall laughed. "I think you're seeing things."

A moment later, he stopped laughing. A person stood in the road in front of them. Rand slammed on the brakes. As the vehicle skidded to a stop on the slick surface, it became clear what stood before them was no human. They faced a strange-looking coyote standing on two legs with multi-colored fur. He looked closer, the coyote seemed to be wearing furs. It snarled, revealing long teeth. Duke found himself climbing out of the Willys. Trembling, he drew his Colt M1911.

The creature looked him up and down with green, glowing eyes, illuminated by the headlight beams. Rand shouted for him to get back in the vehicle. Duke lifted his sidearm. The creature snarled, dropped to all fours, and bounded off the side of the road. Duke tried to track it with his weapon but couldn't see where it went.

The wind whipped by the Willys, causing Duke to shiver.

"Get back in the vehicle!" Rand called. "Let's get out of here."

Duke holstered his weapon with a trembling hand and climbed back in the Willys. He cast one last look over the land-scape. In the distance, he spotted a blue glow. The glow faded and for just a moment, he thought he saw something that resembled a giant soap bubble. He blinked, and it vanished. Duke closed the door. "I lived in Gallup for eighteen years and never saw an animal like that before."

Rand wiped the fog from the front window. "Are you sure we saw what we thought we saw? Maybe it was a skinny bear."

"Bear my foot. That was no human being or animal that I know of. Nothing runs as fast as you were going."

"A cheetah could have paced me," Rand said.

"That was no cheetah or Navajo medicine man." Duke shook his head. "I'm not even sure that was from this Earth. More like the Yuki-onna my grandmother told me about..."

"Or... a skinwalker." Rand wasted no more time. He threw the Willys into gear and accelerated down Route 66 to the comparative safety of Fort Wingate.

CHAPTER FOUR

Tuesday, February 24, 1942

Cheryl arrived home from school just after 4pm, anticipating a nice dinner out and a movie. The change in routine would do her good. She had deliberately avoided considering her feelings about Duke. He may be a real cookie, but he was also about five years younger than her.

She checked the icebox and found some ham and boiled potatoes. Normally, she made dinner each night for her father, but he occasionally worked late and never seemed to mind re-heating dinner for himself. If he didn't arrive home by the time Duke came to pick her up, she'd leave a note.

Entering the bathroom, she applied some fresh makeup, brushed and sprayed her hair, and changed into fresh clothes. Her goal wasn't necessarily to seduce this young man, but she did want to look presentable.

After freshening up, she looked at her watch. It was still only 4:30. She went into the living room and turned on her ham radio, allowing the tubes to warm up. Scanning the channels might seem an unusual hobby for a high school math teacher, especially a woman, but on cloudy days like this, she could pick up signals from far away and that made her feel a little less tied down. Sometimes the set even received broadcasts from England or France, which seemed to transport her to the war.

Although she worried about young men like Duke going into battle, she was glad the United States had finally committed to the effort. Someone needed to put a stop to Adolf Hitler before he took over Europe. She wanted to help if she could. She may not be a fighter, but she had skills in mathematics and electronics and could learn more if given the opportunity. Her mother had taught her Navajo and she took some German in college because so many papers were published in that language.

The lights on the radio illuminated and she put on the headset—around the back of her head, so as not to mess up her hair—and listened. She caught an evangelical show out of Del Rio, Texas, and a radio drama out of Los Angeles. She almost stuck with that last one and listened for a while, but she didn't want to lose track of time. She continued tuning until she heard a lone voice calling out. The words sounded familiar, even though she couldn't hear them clearly.

Her brow furrowed. After a moment, it dawned on her. Someone was broadcasting in Navajo. A burst of static filled the headphones and she held them away from her ears for a moment. When it subsided, she listened again. She tried adjusting the dial slowly first one direction, then the other. Still nothing.

A hand on her shoulder made her jump. She pulled off the headset and whirled around to find her father smiling down at her. He was a big man with thinning blond-gray hair. "Catching anything good on that thing?"

"Mostly the usual. For a moment, I thought I heard someone broadcasting in Navajo, but I lost it and couldn't get it back. It might have been some other language, but I thought I recognized some of the words."

"Someone local?" The sheriff removed his hat and hung it by the door.

Cheryl considered that. "Sounded distant, but in this weather, signal strength can be deceptive, especially if someone has a low-power transmitter, or if I caught a sideband transmission rather than the main signal."

Her father nodded and then looked at her more closely. "You look all dolled up today. I don't smell any cooking either. My great detective skills sense you may have plans for this evening."

"I do, but don't worry, there's cooked ham and potatoes in the icebox. I can reheat them in a jiffy." Cheryl walked to the kitchen.

The sheriff followed. "Don't worry about that. I can fend for myself. I cooked plenty of meals while you were living it up in Las Vegas." He referred to the city north of Santa Fe, New Mexico where New Mexico Normal University was located, not the little town in Nevada busy establishing itself as a kind of western playground. "What I really want to know is who you're stepping out with."

"One of the Marine recruiters in town is taking me to dinner and a show." Cheryl sat down at the table. "Nothing too serious. Just a chance to break the routine a little."

"Which recruiter?" Her dad joined her at the table.

"Duke Ogawa," she said. "You may remember him. He was one of my students my first year back in town."

The sheriff narrowed his gaze. "You're going out with a Japanese boy?"

Cheryl's stomach flip-flopped. She didn't know which word bothered her more, "Japanese" or "boy." She thought back to how Duke had retreated to the background at last night's rally, which made her wonder if he'd encountered pressure to keep a low profile. Even more, she didn't like her dad putting her on the defensive. "What does his ancestry matter? After all, Mom always considered herself an American first even though she was Diné."

Her dad laughed at that. "All right, you've got me there. My dad wouldn't let that go." He shook his head with a smile on his lips, but a hint of sadness around his eyes. "Still, mixed marriages are not something to be considered lightly."

"I'm not talking about marrying Duke, I'm just going with him to dinner and a show, maybe learn a little more about his life in Southern California." She leaned forward. "Besides, I thought you'd be more concerned about me going out with a younger man. After all, he was my student."

Her father leaned forward. "Are you trying to tell me you're eyeing some of your current students as potential husband material?"

She grabbed a hot pad from the table and threw it at him. He caught it out of the air and laughed again.

The doorbell rang. Cheryl jumped to her feet and went to answer the door. Duke stood on the stoop looking handsome in his green winter service uniform. "I hope you don't mind, I dressed down a little for going out to the movies."

Cheryl stifled a laugh at his earnest expression. True, he wasn't in the dress blues he wore to impress the kids at the recruitment rallies, but he still looked dapper with his jacket and tie. In many ways, he looked more dressed up than she was. "You look just fine, Duke."

"And you look ravishing," Duke said with a smile. He stood with his hands behind his back, what soldiers called "at ease" though he didn't seem very relaxed.

"It's cold out there," the sheriff said. "Stop gawking at each other with the door open."

"Please, come in." Cheryl gestured toward the living room.

Duke entered and Cheryl closed the door behind him.

Sheriff Davis looked Duke up and down. "Looks like the Marines have been treating you well, son. Have you had a chance to look up your parents while you've been home?"

"Yes, sir." Duke removed his hat. "We met up on Sunday morning and went to church together."

"Very good." Cheryl's dad nodded approval, then indicated they should take a seat in the living room. "How is the recruitment drive going?"

"It went very well Friday night. A dozen men signed up. I thought this assignment was in the bag, but last night was a bust. It seems everyone's been spooked by Jerry Begay's death." Duke sat down and wrung his hands.

Cheryl continued to stand. She didn't want to get too comfortable and lose track of time.

"Yeah, the Begay kid's death was a damn shame." Cheryl's dad shook his head. "As best as I can tell it was just an unfortunate accident. Could have happened to anyone."

Duke pursed his lips as though he had a question to ask but wasn't certain if he should. He looked at his watch and started to stand, but then kept his seat. "Sheriff, I've been hearing talk about a skinwalker in the area. It seems a lot of the young people are afraid it'll hurt them if they go out at night."

Cheryl gasped. Her knees went weak and she dropped into a chair.

"All a bunch of Navajo nonsense, if you ask me," the sheriff said.

Not nonsense, Cheryl thought, but her throat grew thick and she couldn't speak.

Duke's brow furrowed. "I'm not so sure, sir. Last night, my partner and I..." He hesitated as though trying to find the right words. "We saw a really strange animal. Rand — my partner — thought it might have been the skinwalker we're talking about. It outpaced us as we drove down the highway, then stood in the road right in front of our vehicle."

Cheryl thought her dad would laugh.

"Are you all right?" the sheriff asked.

"Yeah, we're fine, but it sure spooked us."

The sheriff leaned forward. "You're sure it wasn't a rabid coyote?"

"Sir, I've seen plenty of coyotes. I've never seen one stand on two legs before."

The sheriff looked dubious, but he didn't argue. "I'd be surprised if this is some shapeshifting Indian witch, but I'll keep my ear to the ground. If there's a large animal on the loose, that's a real danger. I'll call Fort Wingate if I learn anything useful."

"Sheriff, you're the best," Duke said.

The sheriff turned toward Cheryl. "No, she's the best. You better treat her right or you'll have trouble from me." He stood. "Now you two go and have a good time."

Her dad's words broke her reverie. She pasted on a smile and found her feet again. Duke and the sheriff shook hands, then Duke took Cheryl's elbow and led her to the door.

As Duke and Cheryl entered the Thunderbird Diner he glanced around the restaurant and smiled. One of the things he liked about New Mexico was that he could walk into a restaurant with a white woman and no one paid much attention. He knew New Mexico was far from perfect, though. The situation would be completely different if he were Diné or even black.

The waitress came by and seated them. Duke took a moment to decide what he wanted, then he peeked up over the menu to study Cheryl. He couldn't believe he'd actually asked his one-time teacher out on a date, but she proved just as lovely as long-forgotten fantasies had suggested. Strawberry-blonde hair framed a round, thoughtful face. Nothing about her appearance betrayed the slight difference in their years.

Cheryl noticed him looking. "So, have you decided what you want already?"

Duke cleared his throat and shifted uncomfortably. "Well, I've been missing good Mexican food, so I've been daydreaming about this place's blue corn enchiladas."

"Good choice," Cheryl said with a wink. "but I think I'm going to go with the green chile burger." She narrowed her gaze. "Don't they have Mexican food in California?"

"Oh, they do, but it's not the same thing." He struggled to find words to describe it, with his one-time teacher scrutinizing him.

She laughed at his discomfort, which piqued him for just a moment, but then caused him to relax. The waitress returned, took their orders, and vanished.

"So, can you tell me more about the creature you saw last night?" The question sounded casual, but he thought he detected a certain edge to her tone. He looked around, to see if anyone might be listening. Rand had emphasized how seriously the Diné took skinwalker legends. Speaking of it in a restaurant seemed inappropriate. She probably knew that.

"It was like no creature I'd ever seen. It's long, spindly legs reminded me of a jackrabbit."

She released a nervous chuckle. "Sure you didn't see one of those jackalopes they sell in the curio shops?"

He searched her gaze, trying to decide if she was poking fun at him. As if what he'd seen even remotely resembled a taxidermy rabbit with antlers mounted on its head. Although she'd asked a whimsical question, Cheryl fixed him with an intense gaze. "No, it really looked like an elongated coyote. It's hard to describe, but it's like what would happen if a coyote had a human skeleton inside it." He shook his head. "The head, the paws, the tail were all those of a coyote, but the body was like a person's. And I think it wore clothes, too, or at least had a fur coat besides its natural pelt."

Cheryl's brow furrowed. They fell silent as the waitress brought dinner. When she left, Cheryl shook her head. "And you say this creature ran as fast as the car?"

Duke nodded.

"I don't know what I would have done if I'd seen something like that." She lifted her burger. "I think you're very brave to have kept your cool like you did."

He smiled, seeing no sarcasm or malice in the comment. He hadn't thought he was brave at the time. He remembered just standing there holding the gun. A trained Marine, he should have fired without hesitation. He met Cheryl's blue eyes again and decided to stop analyzing the previous night.

He dug into his enchiladas. They were just as good as he remembered. The spices danced on his tongue and warmed his insides. Somehow, the chile also seemed to calm something within him. It was the perfect meal for a cold winter's evening.

He turned the conversation over to her teaching.

"It's a fine job." Something in her words rang false and didn't quite match his memories of her as someone passionate about mathematics.

"You're not bored already, are you?"

"Not bored, exactly." She shifted under his gaze as though she were now the student. "Just not always challenged in the ways I'd like to be challenged."

Duke laughed. "I thought my classmates gave you plenty of challenges."

She leaned in close. "Trust me, discipline is always a challenge." She sat back and shook her head. "Just not the challenge I signed up for." Her gaze wandered and Duke found himself captivated as she pushed blonde hair behind a gently curving ear. "Sometimes I'm jealous of you, off in the Marines, seeing new places, learning new things…"

"Learning to fight." He feared his words had more of an edge than he intended.

She turned back to him. "I wouldn't be so fond of that part, but it would be nice if I had more choices than being a teacher in Gallup, New Mexico." She arched an eyebrow. "So, can you tell me why you're interested in recruiting Navajos? My mom was Navajo, maybe I have something to offer the war effort."

"I can't tell you and they don't let women in to the Corps." Duke reached out and took her hand. "My great-grandparents were peasant farmers in Japan. When the Meiji Restoration happened, they came to the United States. Now my parents own a feed store here in Gallup." He squeezed her hand. "Me? I'm not sure what I'll do once I get out of the Corps — maybe go to college and get a degree. Maybe I'll be a teacher."

She snorted a laugh.

"The point is, there's no limit to what you can do." He smiled. "You just have to look for the opportunities."

The waitress returned and asked if they wanted dessert. Duke was tempted but looked at his watch. They'd almost stayed too long. He asked for the check. Together, they walked down the street to the theater.

Even on a Tuesday night, the place was packed. Not surprising. Cheryl told him The Wolf Man had just arrived in Gallup. Duke hadn't seen it yet even though it had been released a couple months earlier in San Diego.

As the movie played, Duke's cheeks warmed when Lon Chaney's character spied on Evelyn Ankers with a telescope. He thought it seemed rude and yet it was all too easy to imagine himself doing something similar with Cheryl if given the opportunity. He was glad for the dark theater so she couldn't see his embarrassment as the scene continued on and Chaney flirted with Ankers in the little shop. His embarrassment turned into a chill when Ankers described the werewolf as a human who transformed into a wolf. He knew this was just a movie, but what she described seemed so much like what Rand told him about skinwalkers.

Duke shuddered during the scene where Lon Chaney fought a wolf attacking a friend who accompanied him to the gypsy camp. It looked like a tough fight and he could swear the wolf in the scene was real. It made him glad he hadn't had to fight the creature he'd seen the previous night. He could imagine coming out far worse than the Larry Talbot character did. Cheryl reached over and took his hand. It calmed him a little and made him smile. She had soft skin and he longed to put his arm around her, but feared that would be too forward on a first date.

As the film progressed, he began to see that becoming a werewolf was something of a curse. He wondered if skinwalkers felt that way. Only, Rand had told him Navajo witches deliberately sought skinwalker powers to do evil. Near the film's end, Duke almost laughed when Lon Chaney finally turned into a wolf. He'd seen pictures of the "wolf man" before, so he shouldn't have been surprised, but he clearly looked like a man in a mask. Chaney wasn't anything like the horror he'd seen on the road. Still, the final scene where the wolf man transformed back into Talbot was sobering. What would it be like for a human to change into the creature he'd seen? Did bones change and pop and snap? It made him shudder.

"So, what did you think?" Cheryl asked as the credits rolled. She seemed especially interested in his answer.

"Pretty good film. It made me think." Duke shrugged.

She laughed. "I'm not sure that was the filmmakers' intent."

"No? What about the stars on the cursed men? Doesn't that remind you of the stories about Hitler making Jews wear stars in Germany?"

She smiled at him. "I think there's a good reason you passed your English classes. You clearly understand metaphor." She looked at her watch. "I wish this night could continue on, but I have school to teach tomorrow."

On an impulse, he leaned over and gave her a kiss on the cheek, then started to stand. She held onto his hand and didn't budge. When he turned to face her, she leaned over and gave him a sweet, tender kiss that set his mouth tingling and kept him from thinking about much of anything else for the rest of the night.

Chapter Five

Wednesday, February 25, 1942

A young man named Eddie Pershlakai brushed past Cheryl Davis as she left the supply closet and walked down the hallway. He disappeared into Miss Todachine's classroom. Eddie had graduated two years ago. Cheryl didn't think much about it. He was one of the youths in town the history teacher had helped. A tough guy like Eddie could be a benefit to the Marines — more so than younger boys still in school. A tear rolled down Cheryl's cheek as she thought about Jerry Begay. She brushed it away. Nothing she could do for him anymore.

Cheryl continued down the hall toward her classroom. Frances Todachine and another young man she worked with, John Claw, walked toward her, deep in conversation. Cheryl waved, trying to be friendly. They didn't notice and didn't wave back. She tried not to take it personally but did stop in her tracks. She looked back and watched as they turned into the classroom. If anything, Miss Todachine seemed even more passionate about getting students to succeed than she was. She certainly commanded respect. No teacher — not even Principal Smith — referred to her as Frances.

Cheryl continued toward her room. Another high school graduate passed her in the hall and went toward Miss Todachine's room. Curiosity began to get the better of Cheryl. She stopped in her room and placed the supplies on her desk. Taking just a moment to give them a cursory sort, she then returned to the hallway.

Cheryl strolled down the hall and entered the small supply closet that adjoined Miss Todachine's room. Quietly, she closed the door behind her and didn't turn on the light. A hole in the shared wall allowed sound and light to pass between the rooms. She wasn't certain whether the hole had been for an electrical cable that had been removed or some old gas line, but all the teachers were careful not to make too much noise when visiting the closet to get supplies or Miss Todachine would come out and give them an earful about disturbing her class.

Despite those incidents, Cheryl found it difficult to hear what transpired in the adjoining room. At one point, she thought someone mentioned Jerry Begay.

"Unfortunate," Miss Todachine said. "But..."

Cheryl couldn't make out the rest of the comment.

John Claw's voice came through loud and clear a moment later. "It would serve the white people right to be overrun like we were."

"The actions we take are not about vengeance," Miss Todachine said. "Diné must have power and for too long we have been powerless."

Being a woman and half-Navajo, Cheryl could relate to that.

When the conversation resumed, they spoke Navajo—a language almost no one outside of Northern Arizona and New Mexico knew. Cheryl wondered if the Marines wanted Diné for their language. If she suspected that, she could believe others might as well. It would be a challenging code to break, unless you had Navajo speakers on your side as well. She thought about bringing her concerns to her father, but nothing she heard indicated Axis sympathizers.

She stepped from the closet and came face to face with the principal.

"What were you doing in there with the door closed?" he asked.

"Getting some supplies."

The principal arched an eyebrow and Cheryl realized she hadn't taken anything from the closet.

"Returning some, actually," Cheryl amended. "I picked up more boxes of chalk than I'd intended. Don't want to be wasteful."

He nodded. "Good thinking. Carry on, Miss Davis." Mr. Smith started to walk on but turned around a moment later. "Daisuke Ogawa was in your class about five years ago, wasn't he?"

Cheryl swallowed. "He was. Why do you ask?" She stepped toward the principal.

Mr. Smith frowned. "Probably just loose talk, but someone told the school secretary they saw you kissing Mr. Ogawa down at the El Morro Theatre last night."

She opened her mouth to say something, but the principal held up his hand. "It's none of my business what my teachers do on their personal time, but if there is any truth to this, I advise you to be careful. The city council has been talking about the president's recent executive order. Over in California, the attorney general has said Japanese people cannot assimilate into our culture. I don't buy that, and I don't know what this means for people in the military like our friend Mr. Ogawa. The point is he could have rough days ahead."

Cheryl nodded. "Thank you, sir. I appreciate your concern." With everything else going on, she had almost forgotten about the president's executive order authorizing the detention of people of Japanese descent. It must not have been on Duke's mind much either. Maybe he didn't think people this far into the country would be affected. As her thoughts returned to the present, she realized the principal had already walked away.

Miss Todachine's door opened behind her. Cheryl returned to her classroom, hoping no one had seen her standing there. She finished sorting out the supplies she had brought to the room and then packed up and left.

At home, her thoughts lingered on the previous night with Duke. The kiss they shared had been lovely and she hoped there would be an opportunity for more kisses in the future.

She looked at the clock. Her father would be home soon looking for his supper and she was getting hungry as well. She put two skillets on the stove and prepared to fry up a couple of lamb chops and potatoes.

The front door opened and a few minutes later her dad entered the kitchen. "Smells good in here." He dropped down in a chair at the kitchen table.

"How was your day?" Cheryl asked.

"Ol' Duke's creature encounter made me wonder if there really is some large animal roaming around. A lot of folks, especially Navajos, seem spooked at the moment."

"Don't tell me you think there are witches who can turn into some kind of monster." She flashed a mischievous grin. "I'm the one who went to see the scary movie last night."

"Well, so far I haven't turned up anything. How was your day?"

Cheryl told her dad about the conversation she overheard as she plated the food and brought it to the table. "When I heard someone speaking Navajo on the radio, I began to think it could make a good code language."

"Better not spread that around. If you're right, you could get in trouble." He shrugged. "Even so, it doesn't sound like you heard anything I could investigate." He took a bite and smiled. "Your cooking is every bit as good as your mom's."

"What about Miss Todachine and the men she's always with?"

"You could talk to her. See if she says something concerning. I'm not sure you'd learn anything, but she might let her guard down with you." He concentrated on dinner for a moment, then looked up. "With her connections and understanding of local culture, maybe she knows something about these skinwalker sightings."

Cheryl tensed, then forced herself to relax. "Yes, it would be interesting to find out what she knows."

Her dad finished his dinner, then wiped his mouth with a napkin. "Do you mind if I turn on the radio? I was hoping to catch the latest episode of Red Ryder."

"Only if you help me with the dishes." She collected the plates and took them to the sink. They finished the chore quickly and her father went off to catch his show. She went to her room to do some reading and to think about how she would approach Miss Todachine.

Thursday, February 26, 1942

The phone rang in Sheriff Chuck Davis's office. He picked it up. "Hello."

It was the mayor. "Sheriff, I just received a call from the governor. There's talk that the governor wants to declare Gallup a 'zone of exclusion' as defined by Executive Order 9066."

The sheriff gritted his teeth. "That's the executive order that says Japanese people are to be confined away from military assets."

"That's the one," the mayor said. "Since Fort Wingate is now the storage depot for the western United States, they're saying we need to be on the lookout for spies in this area who might want to get in."

"So, what does this have to do with me?" The sheriff scratched his thinning hairline. "This sounds like a military matter."

"Mostly it is," the mayor admitted, "but they may need your help rounding up people."

Davis considered Duke Ogawa's parents. They were good citizens, and from what he'd seen they raised their boy right. He couldn't imagine people like them being spies. This was a bunch of horse pucky.

"Sheriff, are you still there?"

Davis realized he'd gone silent. He didn't dare say the words that ran through his mind. "Yes, sir, I'm here. What exactly are you asking me to do?"

"There's nothing official yet, all we want is for you to make a list of Japanese people in town and where they live. Not all their last names are obvious, and some have married and have Christian surnames."

What the hell is a Christian surname? Instead of speaking the thought aloud, the sheriff said, "Yes, sir. I'll get one of my deputies on it right away."

"Thank you, Sheriff." With that, the mayor hung up.

As Davis considered who to assign the job, the phone rang again. He thanked God he could delay the task the mayor had dropped in his lap. It would give him some time to think about how to deal with it. Maybe decide if there was a way to convince the city council that following through with any round up of citizens was folly.

"Sheriff Davis," he said into the receiver.

"Sheriff, this is Joe Nez. I live up off of highway 491," said the voice on the other end of the line.

"Yes, Mr. Nez, I've driven out by your place. It's a nice piece of land."

"It's all right. I have enough room for fruit trees and a few head of cattle," the Diné rancher said.

"What can I do for you, Mr. Nez?"

"I went out this morning to feed the cattle and I found one of them dead. Strangest thing I ever seen. I was hoping you could come out and take a look."

Davis's brow furrowed. "Dead cows aren't exactly my department, unless you think it was a poacher." The sheriff grimaced to himself. If it had been a poacher, the rancher would have been calling to report a missing cow, not a dead one.

"If it's a poacher, it's the queerest one I've ever heard about."

"All right, I'll come out and take a look. I'll be there in about half an hour." The sheriff hung up.

He grabbed his hat and coat and told Deputy Martinez at the front desk where he was going. "I should be back in an hour — no more than two."

The deputy nodded and the sheriff climbed in his 1939 Mercury Eight. The sheriff's car was getting on a little, but still got the job done, even driving out along icy highways in the middle of winter. The car was a reliable friend, not unlike Red Ryder's horse in the radio serial he enjoyed.

The sheriff drove through town and turned north on Highway 491. The town's buildings soon fell away, and he drove through rolling grassy countryside with a blue dome of sky overhead. Most of the snow had melted, just leaving craggy knolls dotting the landscape here and there. If he drove long enough, he'd reach Shiprock, a veritable tower of stone.

Twenty minutes later, the sheriff came to the turnoff to Joe Nez's place. He drove five miles along a rutted dirt road. In a few places, the mud threatened to grab onto his tires, but he finally reached a modest, modern ranch house standing near a traditional Navajo hogan. Joe Nez had done well for himself compared to some of the other Diné in the area.

The rancher came out of the house as the sheriff stepped from the car.

"Might as well climb back in, we have another mile to go," Joe said as he climbed in beside the sheriff and pointed to a pair of ruts through the grass.

Davis gritted his teeth, hoping they wouldn't hit a rock large enough to damage his undercarriage. "So, what can you tell me about this dead cow?"

"Eyes and ears gone. Tongue as well." He hesitated. "Ajilchii' cut out."

"Ajilchii'? I don't know that word." The sheriff narrowed his gaze.

"Butt hole," the rancher said. "I don't know the polite word in English."

The sheriff restrained himself from laughing aloud. "It's all right."

It took ten minutes to go the last mile, but finally Joe told the sheriff to stop. They climbed out of the car and he led the way to a spot about ten yards from the road. A cow lay on the ground.

Davis expected blood, gore, and maggots. Instead, his first impression was that the cow had simply lain down and gone to sleep. The only thing that broke the illusion was the empty eye socket staring up at him. Nez knelt down and lifted the cow's head. He showed the sheriff the tongueless mouth. The sheriff walked around the cow. A neat incision had been cut through the cow's nether regions. It might not be a surgically precise wound, but it was butcher-neat. Despite the cold, the sheriff began to sweat. Something about this act seemed unnatural.

"Any ideas who or what would have done this?"

"They say skinwalkers do this to cattle." Joe's expression remained serious. If he was pulling the sheriff's leg, he gave no indication.

Davis walked away from the cow. The cold and the neat incisions kept the odor from being too strong, but the carcass unnerved him. "I've been hearing a lot about skinwalkers the last few days. I even heard a report about a strange, large animal that I am taking seriously." He leaned against the car. "I know you respect the old ways, but you also strike me as levelheaded. I accept that you believe a skinwalker is responsible, but what do you think a skinwalker is?"

"An animal," Joe said, "but not a normal one. Like a bear, they can walk on two legs or four. A normal animal wouldn't kill so cleanly. I don't know why any animal would have such specific tastes."

The sheriff breathed out a sigh. "I doubt this is the work of an animal. If I had to guess, I'd say this is the work of someone out to scare you. This looks like a prank, not an animal attack. Have you annoyed anyone that you know of?"

Joe shook his head. "Only people I've talked to are some of the kids who come and help me out on the ranch. Some of 'em are thinking about going off and joining the Marines. I may have lost my temper at them. It seemed like they were taking the first opportunity they could to abandon their families."

"I think they actually want to help out. They'd get good pay and they'd be doing their part to keep the country safe."

"Maybe, but I do my part by keeping the ranch operational. I won't be able to do that if all the young people leave."

"All right." The sheriff decided not to get into an argument. He put his hands on his hips. "If this is an animal, my best advice is to set out some traps, see if you catch it."

"What if it is a prankster, like you suggest?"

"Hopefully, they're smart enough to stay out of the traps."

Joe nodded. "Some of my people say skinwalkers have a way of transforming themselves from human to animal."

The sheriff narrowed his gaze. "Do you think there's any truth to that?"

"I've been out here on this ranch for a lotta years." Joe's gaze drifted to the horizon. "I think there are many things about this world we don't completely understand. I think there are a lot of animals that know how to avoid traps, too." He paused and looked back toward the cow's carcass. "There's one more thing I forgot to point out. When I first discovered the carcass, I looked for footprints. I didn't see a thing."

The sheriff walked back and looked around. Lots of rock and scrub, but he could make out his boot prints where he'd walked around the carcass with the rancher. Someone careful or with a light step could avoid leaving tracks. He returned to the car. "All I can suggest is, set out traps. If it's an animal, try to capture it."

The two climbed back in the car and the sheriff drove the rancher back to his house.

Chapter Six

Thursday, February 26, 1942

Sheriff Chuck Davis knew his daughter had a free class period at the end of the school day. He was now much more curious about this Miss Todachine and the young men she spent time with. If they were intimidating people or deliberately scaring people, he wanted that stopped. If the cattle mutilation wasn't a random act by a large animal, but a person destroying property, it was his business. He had no leads other than a teacher who worked with students who had a history of causing trouble. If any of that crowd were the kids Joe Nez had yelled at, that could explain a lot. Of course, even as that thought crossed his mind, he realized most of these alleged troublemakers had been rather quiet since Miss Todachine came to town. Maybe he was barking up the wrong tree.

The sheriff drove back to Gallup. When he arrived in town, he glanced at his watch. He still had half an hour until his daughter got out of class, so he drove over to the Thunderbird Diner to grab some coffee and a slice of pie.

A Navajo waitress named Doreen served him. "What do you know, Doreen?" he asked with a polite smile.

"Not much, Sheriff. Things have been quiet. It's like the cold weather has frozen everything in place." Doreen never smiled back. The sheriff liked that she didn't try to hide her feelings behind a false front.

"Did you hear about the Marines in town trying to recruit new soldiers?" He sat back. "I heard they had a lot of luck on Friday night."

"The storm over the weekend chilled their enthusiasm. That and Jerry Begay's death." She shook her head. "He was a good kid."

"I could use some coffee and pie against this chill." After placing the order, the sheriff cocked his head to get a better look at Doreen's face. "Any chance something besides the cold air is damping people's enthusiasm?"

"Maybe. I've heard some whispers."

"What kind of whispers?"

She looked around before answering. "I think you've heard the stories about the skinwalker."

"Do you think skinwalkers are real?"

"I think they scare people so much there wouldn't be talk unless there was one around..." She trailed off.

"Could someone pretend to be one?" The sheriff narrowed his gaze.

"Maybe, but they would be playing a dangerous game. Anyone doing that must want something important." She turned to leave, then looked back. "Apple pie, right?"

The sheriff nodded. Then he called out after her, "And a piece to go for Cheryl."

He thought he caught a hint of a smile as she went back to the kitchen.

He contemplated Doreen's words as he ate his pie and sipped his coffee. A war secret could be important. So could a rancher's lost revenue. He made sure to leave Doreen a big tip, then drove over to the school.

He knocked on the doorframe of Cheryl's classroom and peered around the corner. She looked up from her writing and smiled.

Davis returned her smile and handed her the pie.

"Why, thank you," Cheryl said, her smile deepening.

"I was just wondering if you had a chance to speak to Miss Todachine yet?"

Cheryl shook her head. "No, I was going to do that after I finished this lesson plan."

Davis nodded. "Mind if I go with you?"

"I'd like the company." She returned to her work. A few minutes later, she finished and closed the notebook. "All done for today?"

Davis nodded to his daughter and the two walked down the hall to Miss Todachine's classroom. The sheriff knocked. When he didn't receive an answer, he opened the door. The lights were off.

"This is her free period, too. She must have gone home already," Cheryl said.

The sheriff turned on the light. Cheryl gasped. Davis looked at the chalkboard. Someone had drawn a swastika. Next to it was a map. The sheriff recognized it as the Navajo Nation. Some points had been marked and labeled. One mark was labeled Gallup, another was Shiprock. Some points weren't labeled. An "x" had been drawn a little north of Gallup, about where Joe Nez's ranch was located. Another "x" was near a place called Standing Rock. Nothing much out there but a few homes and a meeting place for the Tse'ii'ahi' clan. Still, Davis made a mental note.

"What does it all mean?" Cheryl's brow furrowed.

"I think it means I have a good reason to go speak with Miss Todachine and I might have to go for a drive after dinner." The sheriff took out a notepad and did his best to copy the map.

"Do you want me to go with you?" Cheryl asked.

The sheriff shook his head. "No. I'll go on my own for this." They left the classroom, and the sheriff gave his daughter a quick kiss on the forehead, then stopped in the front office to ask about Miss Todachine's address.

Nice part of town, he thought as he walked back to his car. He wondered how she could afford a house in that neighborhood on a teacher's salary. He cautioned himself not to think about that too hard. After all, he didn't know who her relatives were. Cheryl lived in a nicer house than she could probably afford, courtesy of being the sheriff's daughter.

He drove over and pulled up in front of the history teacher's house. He shuddered as he looked at the imposing red brick façade. He noticed a large antenna, not unlike the one Cheryl had installed for her ham radio set.

He left the car and knocked on the door. He wasn't sure what he expected from the descriptions of Miss Todachine as a do-gooder who worked with troubled youth. He was surprised when a woman under five-feet-tall answered the door. He guessed she was about the same age as his daughter with clear skin and dark brown—almost black—eyes.

"May I help you, officer?" She had a deep, steady voice, which made the sheriff think it should belong to a more mature woman.

The sheriff introduced himself. "I just had a couple of questions. There have been some strange… incidents around town. I know you work with some of the young people. I thought it was possible some of them might know something."

She considered that for a moment, then nodded. "What kind of strange incidents?"

"May I come in? It's rather cold out here."

She narrowed her gaze but gave a curt nod. She opened the door and he entered. He glanced around at modest, handmade furnishings.

"You may know there have been some recruiters for the Marine Corps in town."

"Yes, I was at their recruitment rally last Friday night."

The sheriff nodded. "That rally garnered a lot of enthusiasm, but it's all waned. I've heard people are afraid to enlist now. The root of the problem is that some people seem to have been the subject of dangerous pranks."

She lifted her eyebrows. It seemed like genuine surprise. "Pranks? What kinds of pranks?"

The sheriff held up his hand. "I can't to go into details. You know a lot of young people with troubled histories. I just wanted to ask whether you've heard anything about this."

She shook her head. "I've heard nothing about people committing pranks." She maintained a straight face and didn't show any sign of lying that he could detect.

"I dropped by your classroom this afternoon to speak with you there." He shrugged and again took the opportunity to glance around. "I thought it would be less invasive than visiting you at your home. I was surprised to see a swastika on your chalkboard."

Miss Todachine smiled. "It's a traditional Native American symbol. I can't help it if men like Adolf Hitler have absconded with it."

The sheriff knew that but found it interesting she was a little defensive about Hitler. "Would it be possible for you to ask the young men you work with about these pranks?"

"Do you think they're responsible?" She jumped on his question.

"Not necessarily, but you've helped them find jobs around town, haven't you? They may have heard something."

"Of course," The teacher gestured toward the door. "Now, if you'll excuse me, I have plans for this evening."

"Yes, ma'am. Thank you for your time." The sheriff returned to his car and drove home.

He found Cheryl had already fried up some ham and made some mashed potatoes for dinner along with some green beans. The sheriff ate and wiped his mouth. "That was wonderful as always. You should let me do the cooking once in a while."

"If I let you do the cooking, I wouldn't eat until after eight o'clock those days." She winked at him and picked up the dishes. "I'd starve!"

"At least let me wash the dishes tonight," the sheriff said. "After that, I want to go take a drive and I may be out late."

"Oh, where are you going?"

Davis stood and took the dishes from his daughter. He put them in the sink and drew the water. "Out to Standing Rock." As he spoke the words, he knew the marked locations on the chalkboard could have been coincidence. Perhaps Frances Todachine had been teaching the students something about Navajo history. Crude marks on a chalkboard weren't much to go on.

"Would you like some company?" Cheryl removed her apron and hung it on a rack. "My lessons are ready for tomorrow. I didn't have anything planned except for scanning the radio channels."

The sheriff considered her offer. It tempted him. After all, the worst he expected to encounter were some young men out making mischief. He could handle that, even if they turned rowdy or decided to make trouble. As he washed the dishes, he considered all the things that had happened the last few days and realized there might be a way for his daughter to help out.

"Cat got your tongue?" Cheryl prompted when her father hadn't answered.

"Sorry." He looked over his shoulder and smiled. "Just thinking." He rinsed the last glasses, then turned around. "Remember the other night when you picked up those strange signals on your ham radio? It might be most useful to me if you can monitor the bands where you picked them up. See if you can get something stronger, find out what they're saying."

Cheryl narrowed her gaze. "Do you have a reason to suspect they'll be transmitting tonight? Even though I thought I heard Navajo, there's no good reason to think that was a local broadcast."

Davis shook his head. "I'm operating entirely on hunches and guesses here. Ol' Basil Rathbone would not be impressed with my methods." He referred to the Sherlock Holmes radio serials his daughter enjoyed listening to.

"All right. I'll tune in and give it a listen." Her chipper smile became a concerned frown. "I actually was curious if there's been any more word about the president's executive order concerning Japanese people."

Davis bit back a grimace. He could have done without the reminder of the mayor's unpleasant task. He wanted to tell her about the phone call, but thought it would be inappropriate, plus it would only worry her more. "Duke is pretty special to you, isn't he?"

Cheryl sighed and shrugged. "I don't know whether he's boyfriend material or not, but I do like him and care about him. I don't want to see him or his family hurt."

"Neither do I." He walked over to her and patted her on the shoulder. "Give the radio a listen. I have a feeling that might be the best way to help Duke."

She reached out and hugged her father. Davis felt a warm glow inside. He loved his daughter and wanted to make sure she was happy. A lump formed in his throat as he thought about Cheryl's mother. The sheriff gave his daughter a squeeze, then he went to the door, grabbed his warm coat and hat, and returned to the car.

The sun had already set. A few stars and the gibbous moon appeared in the twilight sky. He thought a full moon would be more helpful for poking around at night, but three-quarters of a moon would have to do. He climbed into the Mercury and turned the ignition. The big car roared to life despite the bitter cold.

He drove through town and took Highway 491 north. Everything looked different at night. It wasn't just the lack of light, but the shadows made different features of the landscape stand out.

He drove for a while longer, thinking about the map. There was no reason to suspect any troublemakers would show up in Standing Rock this particular night but he had so little to go on he had to follow every possible lead. Still, his odds of learning something from this trip were slim. Davis was so absorbed in his thoughts, he almost missed his turnoff. He made a hard right and the Mercury fishtailed. Looking around, he was glad no one else was driving along the highway to see him execute such a clumsy turn.

He pulled up to the chapterhouse in Standing Rock and was surprised to see a few cars in the parking lot. Yeitso Begay walked out of the building and approached the sheriff's car. He recognized the man as an area clan leader and, Davis gathered, a distant cousin of Jerry Begay's family.

The sheriff rolled down the window.

"What brings you out this way, Sheriff?" Begay asked.

The sheriff killed the engine. "Just a hunch, my friend." He reached through the window and the two men shook hands. "What's going on tonight?"

Begay shrugged. "Just a clan council meeting. It's wrapping up." Indeed, a few more men left the building and climbed into their vehicles.

"Have you seen any strange activity around here? Any young people causing trouble? Strange animal attacks?"

Begay pursed his lips. "Nothing like that. Just the cold weather and the war in Europe. People asked me if I thought there was anything mysterious in my cousin's death. I told them I didn't think so. I encouraged a few of them to talk to their families, go listen to what the Marines have to say. They're having another meeting on Friday, right?"

"They are," Davis affirmed.

"Good. I heard one of them is a Yazzie from Show Low. They're good people. They're related to my wife's family."

"Well, listen." Davis leaned out the window. "If anything strange happens, give me a call in Gallup. I want to know about it. I have a feeling there are some troublemakers trying to discourage kids from signing up."

Begay looked as though he wanted to say something but stopped himself. He nodded. "I'll do that, Sheriff." Again, the two men shook hands. Begay went up to the building and spoke to another man shutting off the light. The two climbed into separate cars and drove away.

The sheriff sat in his car deciding what to do. The night had proved unexpectedly productive and he thought maybe he should just turn around and drive home, so he could get some good sleep.

Then he caught some movement out of the corner of his eye. He climbed out of the car and looked around. A light breeze blew, rustling the grass nearby. He stood and listened a little longer. He thought he heard something like a yip and a faint growl from the direction of a shadowy mesquite bush.

He pulled his revolver and walked in that direction.

A creature rose up from behind the bush. The top of its head easily matched his six feet. Long ears made it almost a foot taller. It barred its teeth.

The sheriff fought to keep his wits about him and study the creature. Did it wear a necklace? Hard to tell in the pale moonlight. It might have a concho belt as well, but maybe that was just the coloring of its pelt. The head, paws, and tail were clearly those of a coyote. The body… He thought of a tall, skinny boy.

Saliva dripped from the creature's jaws as it growled.

The sheriff leveled his revolver and fired as the creature leapt straight up and over the bush.

A bright flash of light burst through the air and a shockwave knocked the sheriff onto the dirt road. His head hit on a rock with a thud, but he still maintained consciousness long enough to see the flash congeal into something like a glowing soap bubble, which zoomed off into the distance.

CHAPTER SEVEN

Thursday, February 26, 1942

Sheriff Chuck Davis woke up shivering. He tried to remember what he was doing on the ground under a starlit sky. Then he remembered the horrifying vision of the creature standing before him, followed by a bright flash. Or was that him falling and knocking himself out? He sat up and reached for the back of his head. His hand came away clean. He checked his watch by the light of the moon. Only a few minutes had passed since he'd left the car.

Grabbing his hat, which lay nearby, he stood. A little woozy, he stumbled over to the car and held on until the world stopped spinning. He was both glad he had not allowed his daughter to accompany him and regretting the choice. She might have been in danger, but she could have driven him home afterward. Glancing toward the chapterhouse, he saw phone lines. If needed, he might be able to get in and call for help.

His head began to clear, and he reached inside his car's glove compartment for a flashlight. He walked over to where the creature had been. Finding the exact spot proved easy. The mesquite brush had been blackened by whatever caused the flash. A pair of clean tracks stood in the middle of the blackened earth. They resembled dog or coyote tracks, but these were the biggest coyote prints he'd ever seen. A short trail of the tracks led away from the burned area and disappeared on more gravelly terrain.

He returned to the car and tucked the flashlight under his chin so he could write. He noted down everything he'd seen. What he'd seen had been no ordinary animal. He'd also begun to wonder whether the creature people reported was just someone in a costume—maybe even a Navajo dance costume. A scared person seeing someone dressed like a coyote with a realistic head dress might imagine it being more animal than human.

Only, he couldn't rationalize what he'd seen so easily. The tracks especially seemed to clinch it. The sheriff frowned, looked at his watch again, and decided he felt good enough to drive home. As he drove, he pondered the flash and the vision of the creature disappearing into a bubble and floating away. A person perpetrating a hoax could easily have dropped a flash bomb. That would explain the burned bush and ground. But for the life of him, he couldn't explain away the glowing bubble. He should have looked harder for additional evidence. Then again, someone good enough to leave convincing coyote tracks probably wouldn't leave behind any more evidence than they intended.

If the skinwalker were a prankster, it certainly wasn't Miss Todachine. The creature he'd seen had been much taller than the little woman. Then he remembered a circus that came to town when he was a kid. One of the acts that had captivated him had been a stilt walker. He released a derisive snort at his own train of thought. Although he could imagine stilts manufactured to leave coyote tracks, he couldn't imagine anyone balancing on them long enough to produce the tracks he'd seen. He also figured he wouldn't so easily mistake a man or woman on stilts for a living, snarling creature. He'd seen teeth and saliva dripping down fur-covered jaws. He shuddered as he pulled into the driveway in front of his house.

Cheryl had left the porch light on for him. He went inside the dark house, turned off the light, then trudged to his room to get some sleep. He tossed and turned for a long time, finding it difficult to get comfortable. Although he hadn't broken skin in his fall, an uncomfortable lump had certainly formed. Also, he couldn't get the image of the creature out of his mind.

Friday, February 27, 1942

The alarm bell rang all too early. The sheriff must have fallen asleep. He climbed out of bed, prepared for his day, and went into the kitchen where the scents of bacon and coffee greeted him, making him smile despite the lingering darkness outside. Cheryl brought him a plate and kissed him on the cheek. "You were out late last night. I didn't hear you come in."

"It was quite a night." Davis wrestled with how many details to give her. "I think I saw the creature Duke told us about."

Cheryl bit her lip and walked around behind her father. "You didn't get in a fight with it, did you?" Her voice quavered.

"Nothing like that." The sheriff turned and flashed her a reassuring smile. "I just stumbled in the dark."

While her father told her what happened, Cheryl chipped off some ice, folded it into a towel, and handed it to him.

"So, you believe there really is a skinwalker?" she declared at last.

Davis shrugged. "It's a physical creature, yes. Is it somehow an elaborate prank? I hope so, but I don't know how they pulled it off."

"You should have let me come with you last night."

"I'm not sorry I didn't take you." He sipped his coffee. Actually, the second set of eyes might have helped him analyze what had happened, but given the danger, he was just as glad she hadn't been there.

By the time he finished breakfast, the ice Cheryl had chipped into the washcloth had melted. He took the towel to the sink and wrung it out. He kissed his daughter goodbye, grabbed his hat from beside the door, and stepped outside just as the sun rose.

He drove into the sheriff's office and unlocked the door. It wasn't uncommon for him to be the first to arrive. As he walked back toward his office, the phone at the front desk rang. The sheriff answered.

"Sheriff? This is Joe Nez."

"Good morning, Mr. Nez. How are you?"

The rancher paused for a moment. "I'm okay, but perplexed. I set out traps like you suggested. When I woke up this morning, I found the one closest to my house triggered. It hadn't caught anything. I checked a few of the other traps near the house. They were all the same."

The sheriff rubbed the back of his neck. "Any tracks?"

"Yeah, lots of them. They looked like coyote, but they were the biggest damn coyote tracks I'd ever seen."

The sheriff moved around the desk, trying not to tangle the phone cord. He sat down. "If a coyote sprang your traps, is there any chance it could have gotten away?"

"These were bear traps. They would have killed any ordinary coyote."

The sheriff leaned forward, as though asking the next question in confidence. "Any signs that something burned near the traps?"

Nez went silent for another moment. "Now that you mention it, the grass around two of the traps did look burned."

The sheriff had a vision of a magical monster that could turn into a soap bubble and float away on the wind. "Any blood or hair on the traps?"

"No blood," Nez said. "There were some hairs on one of the traps. Looked like dog or coyote hair to me. Kind of yellowish, like a coyote or a golden retriever."

The sheriff shuddered, then thanked the rancher for calling.

"I think you should give more of the presentation tonight," Randall Yazzie said as he drove to Gallup from Fort Wingate.

Duke looked out at the passing scenery. The weather had improved as the week progressed. Most of the snow had melted. "It wasn't your presentation that kept people from signing up. You were terrific on Monday night and we've had a lot of people sign up in Farmington and Grants."

"But you're the local boy," Rand urged. "I can only bring them so far. You're the one who grew up with them. You're the one who has the Bengal pride..."

"Tiger pride," Duke interjected.

Rand snorted. "That's what I mean. I can talk about patriotism, opportunities, and kicking Hitler's hiney up one end of the Rhine and down the other, but you're the one who makes this personal for the folks you grew up with. Besides, we could really use more Navajo speakers for the Code Talker program."

"I still don't think my sitting on the sidelines is what kept people from signing up on Monday night." Duke turned to face Rand. "People are scared."

"And you know what, you faced the monster and you're still here to tell the tale." Rand cast a sidelong glance at Duke.

"So did you."

"But I'm Diné. We talk about skinwalkers in whispers when no one else is listening," Rand urged.

"So, I'm the Japanese boy who's supposed to shock them with my talk?"

"Keep it vague," Rand suggested. "You can be subtle. I believe in you."

Duke looked out the window as they reached the outskirts of town. "So, what about Colonel Barr? He won't be happy if word gets back to him about me speaking after he warned us."

"So what?" Rand shrugged. "He's not our CO and we'll be leaving on Monday. What's he going to do? Give you a stern talking to?"

"He could send a report back to our CO. If they do round up people of Japanese ancestry, it could make trouble for me down the road." Duke looked out the front window. They were approaching the high school much too fast for his comfort.

"If we get recruits tonight, I'm sure our CO will weigh that against anything an army colonel babysitting an arms depot has to say about you." Rand turned into the school parking lot.

"All right." Duke gave a curt nod. "I'll say a few words."

"That's the Bengal spirit!" Rand parked the vehicle.

"Tiger spirit." Duke gave a roar and the two laughed. They climbed out of the Willys MB and grabbed their papers. The principal met them at the gym's entrance and helped them set up tables in the foyer, then led them into the gym itself. Duke was pleased to see the bleachers already about a quarter full.

His stomach sank when Miss Todachine arrived once more, surrounded by a group of tough-looking Navajo men. They climbed about halfway up the left side and found seats. Didn't she have anything better to do on a Friday night? He knew he'd be called in to Colonel Barr's office tomorrow no matter how well things went this night.

More people filed in and took seats. It seemed the improved weather brought more people out and either they'd shaken off their fears of the skinwalker or they didn't really believe them. Duke's heart soared when Cheryl entered. She smiled and waved, then climbed up to a seat high on the right side. His lips tingled as he remembered that kiss in the theater after watching The Wolf Man. He'd wanted to howl like Lon Chaney. His only regret was that he had to leave on Monday. How long would it be before he returned to Gallup? What if he was sent overseas? Would he come back?

The principal stood up and made his introductory remarks, then Randall stepped up to the mic and gave another polished presentation. Duke thought he got better each time. As Rand spoke, Duke's thoughts drifted back to Cheryl.

"I'd like to introduce my friend, Daisuke 'Duke' Ogawa, who calls Gallup home."

Duke blinked back surprise. Was it already time for him to speak? He stepped up to the microphone and started simply. He told the crowd how his parents moved to town and started a feed store. They didn't have much and the Marine Corps allowed him to send money home to help them out.

"I know some of you are scared of going overseas and leaving your families. You feel like a dark specter is stalking you." Duke avoided looking toward Miss Todachine. Instead, he looked up toward Cheryl. "The other night, I caught The Wolf Man down at the El Morro. The unknown can be like that, but it's fantasy. It's all there to scare you until you turn on the lights. Just the other night, after leaving the gym, my buddy and I saw a big coyote running alongside the road. I tell you, it sure spooked us, but when we got out of the car and faced it down, it took off." He clapped his hands once and made a whoosh sound. This time he did look toward Miss Todachine. She glared at him. Despite that, he couldn't imagine her with sharpened teeth dripping saliva. Now some of the young men with her… He dropped the thought, smiled, then handed the microphone over to Rand. As he sat down, a light murmur buzzed through the crowd. Had he gone too far?

He turned to look up toward Cheryl. Her smile from the stands cheered him. Even if he lost people, she still believed in him. It didn't matter what happened at this point.

Before he knew it, the rally came to an end. Rand grabbed some papers and nudged Duke. The two walked out to the foyer.

By the time they had the forms out, young men had lined up. It wasn't quite the crowd they had a week ago, but they signed up several new recruits. Duke and Rand told them the bus would arrive on Monday to take them to Fort Wingate where they would be sworn in. They'd fill out paperwork, then leave on the train that night.

A Navajo man with long hair and corded muscles, wearing a tight shirt stepped up. "Is this where I volunteer?" His words sounded like a dare.

Duke thought he recognized the man as one of the people sitting with Miss Todachine. "Yes, it is." The sign-up was a simple procedure. Duke finished by handing the man a mimeographed sheet of paper with instructions telling him what to bring.

He narrowed his gaze. "What if I don't show up on Monday?"

"What you've signed is called an enlistment contract," Rand explained. He'd already said words to that effect during the signup process, but he took it slow. "You can change your mind before the bus comes on Monday by calling me or Duke at Fort Wingate. We'll try to convince you otherwise, but you can back out without any ramifications."

"That's not what I asked," The man leaned down. "I asked what if I don't show up?"

Duke flashed a winning smile. "Then Uncle Sam will be knocking on your door in a few weeks."

"Like he did with my ancestors," the recruit grumbled.

"You thinking about skipping out?" Rand sat back and folded his arms.

"Nah, just curious." He stepped away and let the next person approach.

Duke looked down at the contract. The man had signed "John Claw." He thought he remembered that name. He was two years behind him in high school.

Duke and Rand signed up two more recruits. When the line cleared, the only other people in the foyer were Principal Smith and Cheryl. Duke stood up from the table and walked to Cheryl. He took her hands. "May I walk you out to your car?"

When she didn't respond, he followed her gaze back to the principal, who seemed to be watching them carefully.

"I can make it out on my own, thanks," she said.

The principal seemed satisfied and went into the gym, probably to have a word with the janitors putting away tables.

"Is everything okay?" Duke asked.

"Oh, it's fine, but you know how people like to talk."

Duke sighed. "I know that. I was wondering if you'd like to go out again tomorrow. I'm in a mood to celebrate our success tonight."

Her smile beamed. "I thought you wouldn't ask. Yes. I'd be delighted and I think my dad would like to talk to you a little more."

Duke's stomach twisted a little at that, but he nodded. He did like Cheryl's dad, but he felt like the sheriff had scrutinized him a little too carefully. "See you tomorrow at six?"

Cheryl nodded. She squeezed his hands and leaned over, giving him a quick peck on the cheek, then stepped out into the cold night. Duke walked back over to the table.

"So, is this getting serious?" Rand asked.

Duke shrugged. "I'm not sure yet, but it is pretty nice."

CHAPTER EIGHT

Saturday, February 28, 1942

After breakfast, Duke Ogawa checked out a Willys MB from the Fort Wingate motor pool. It was one of the privileges Colonel Barr had granted the two Marine recruiters from California. As long as they had no other duties and the vehicles weren't otherwise needed, they could check out a Willys to drive the fifteen miles into town.

Saturday proved a crisp, clear morning. Duke appreciated the chance to have a day off. He glanced around at the view as he drove into Gallup. The drive started out on flat land, but dramatic red rocks stood in the distance. The Atchison, Topeka, and Santa Fe train chugged along the tracks, a thick cloud of black smoke trailing along its length.

With a clear highway, it only took him about thirty minutes to make the drive from the fort into town. He drove down Main Street, lined with brick and block storefronts side-by-side. Duke smiled as he noticed one in particular: Ogawa Feed. The lights were on inside. He remembered many afternoons going there after school. In elementary school, he'd sit in the back and do homework. Once finished, his dad put him to work stocking shelves and helping customers. He'd kept up the routine through high school.

He turned down a nearby street and pulled up in front of a small three-bedroom ranch house with a pitched roof. The roof had been flat when they moved in, but his dad had it redone. "Gallup gets too much snow," he had said.

Duke went to the door and let himself in. When he had visited the previous weekend, he had rung the bell, but his mother chastised him. "It's still your house, let yourself in."

He removed his hat and took a moment to look around. The house contained little to remind him of his Japanese heritage. In fact, his grandparents had brought little aside from the clothes they wore when they left Japan. Still, the familiar smells enveloped him like a warm blanket, and he wished he could stay. Even more, he hoped no one would try to take this place away from his parents. He walked through the living room and entered the kitchen, where his dad read the newspaper and his mom washed the breakfast dishes.

"Duke, good to see you," his dad said. "Come and sit."

"Did you have breakfast?" his mom asked.

"I did, thanks." Duke thought about the watery scrambled eggs and slimy hash browns he had eaten and wished he'd delayed breakfast until he reached town, but he'd been hungry. He stepped over and hugged his mom, then sat at the kitchen table.

"It sounds like bad business near Java," Kenji Ogawa said. Although he had a Japanese given name, he went by Ken around town. "The allies lost five ships."

Duke's stomach churned and he knew it was more than greasy hash browns.

Duke's mom, Mariko, who went by Mary, put her hand to her chest and dropped into a seat near Duke. "Are you sure they're not going to send you out into the Pacific?"

Duke took his mom's hand and gave it a firm squeeze. "I'm a recruiter. They need me stateside." He tried to put more conviction into that than he felt. He also couldn't help but feel that many of the young men he recruited would be going into those fights his dad read about in the paper.

"How did the recruiting drive go last night?" Ken asked. He folded the paper and set it aside.

"We signed up nine new recruits. We have twenty to take back to California from Gallup. Ten will be coming down from Farmington and we have twenty-three recruits from Grants."

"Did the Ito boy turn up?" Dan Ito had taken over in the feed store after Duke had left.

"Yes, he did. He seems like he's grown into a good, strong kid." Duke remembered the scrawny kid who seemed obsessed with Flash Gordon and Tarzan serials.

"Lifting bags of feed grain will do that to you." Ken winked. "Didn't seem to do you any harm either."

"Twenty kids from Gallup doesn't sound like much," Mary said. "Are your superiors satisfied?"

Duke shrugged. "It's still the early days of the war. It feels a long way away for a lot of people here in New Mexico." He considered the secret part of his mission, the special interest in recruiting young men who spoke Navajo. They'd done well on that score, though not quite as well as he'd hoped. "We've done what they asked us. Between our recruits from Farmington, Grants, and Gallup, we'll fill a train car going to California."

"I worry that a train carload won't come home." Mary dabbed the corner of her eye with a napkin.

Duke quickly changed the subject. "To be honest, I'm more worried about you here in Gallup. Have you read the news about the president's executive order?"

Ken nodded. "Yes, but it sounds like they're mostly interested in rounding up Japanese people."

Duke shook his head. "From what I hear, it's not just Japanese citizens, they're worried about anyone with Japanese ancestry."

Ken leaned forward. "Really? They can't be serious. I don't even know anyone in Japan. We have no connections and even if we did, my loyalties are to the United States."

"I know, but people are scared, and scared people don't always think clearly." Duke nodded and sighed. "Especially when losses keep happening in places like the Pacific."

"What would they do with the store if they took us away? What would they do with the house?" Mary's eyes darted from side to side, as though she watched for people marching on them this very moment.

"I have no idea, but maybe it would be good to talk to people around town," Duke suggested. "Maybe you should make arrangements for their care should something happen."

"You don't think they'll come in the middle of the night like those Nazis in Germany?" Mary's eyes locked on her son.

"Mom, if they did that, I don't know what I'd do." Duke stood up and began pacing. He looked down at his uniform coat. "Today, I feel proud of this uniform. If that happened..." He trailed off. He was a Marine. He couldn't just resign and walk away.

Ken nodded and changed the subject. "What are your plans for today?"

"I thought I'd spend time here until this afternoon. Maybe go through the books in my room and pick one or two to take back with me." His shoulders relaxed and he returned to his seat at the table. "This evening, I was going to take Cheryl Davis out to dinner."

"She's the sheriff's daughter, isn't she?" Ken flashed a slight smile.

"She was your teacher, wasn't she?" Mary narrowed her gaze.

Duke laughed and held up his hands. For a moment, he almost wished he had kept his plans as secret as the Navajo language program. He looked at his mom. "She's only five years older than I am. I was her student the first year she taught." He turned to his dad. "Yes, she's the sheriff's daughter. I've visited with Chuck Davis. He's a good man."

Ken pointed to the newspaper he'd been reading. "There was a story that said the sheriff is trying to track down some wild animal. Joe Nez told me it killed one of his cows. You've been driving back and forth a lot. Seen anything?"

Duke thought about the incident the other night on Route 66. "I think we may have seen it, but it ran off before we got a good look." He didn't want to say more and spook his mother. Instead, he asked to see the article. The article said nothing about a skin-walker, which didn't surprise him. It just sought information about a large animal reported to have killed cattle on area ranches.

Duke lost interest in the article and handed the paper back to his dad. He found himself more focused on Cheryl and his hope they would get to share another electrifying kiss.

Duke spent the rest of the morning with his parents. After that, he drove to a florist shop on Main Street then over to Cheryl's house, which reminded him of some homes in San Diego's Gaslamp district, but seemed out of place in rural New Mexico.

Duke grabbed the flowers from the seat beside him, then went up to the door and knocked. His stomach knotted when the sheriff answered. The big man smiled and reached out as though to take the flowers. "For me?"

Duke's eyes widened and the sheriff laughed. The recruiter thought it uncanny how much father and daughter actually resembled one another once you looked closely. He stammered and tried to say they were for Cheryl.

"Oh, I know who the flowers are for and I know you want to give them to her yourself." The sheriff motioned for Duke to come inside. "Cheryl will be out in a moment." He indicated a seat next to a small table.

Duke set the flowers down on the table while the sheriff took a seat on the couch across from him.

"I hear that last night's recruitment drive went better," Davis said.

"It did, sir. We now have a total of twenty recruits from Gallup. My partner, Randall Yazzie, was going to wire our CO today. We suspect he'll be pleased." Deep down, Duke felt a pang of disappointment. He'd been certain they would be able to entice at least forty recruits from Gallup and the first night had convinced him he should have been able to have achieved his goal.

"That's good, that's good." Davis sounded distracted. He leaned forward. "Have you seen the strange animal again since your encounter on Monday night?"

Duke shuddered at the memory of the creature. "No, sir. I'm glad to say I haven't." He didn't want to admit that each time he drove Route 66 between Gallup and Fort Wingate at night, he watched for the creature. He was glad the ice and snow had melted. It allowed him to go a little faster along the highway than he might have normally.

"I know what you mean," the sheriff said. "As it turns out, I saw it on Thursday night." He shook his head and rubbed his hands. "I keep trying to convince myself it was a person in a suit or some clever, trained animal..."

"Sir, what I saw was no person in a suit. That animal ran over forty miles an hour, then jumped and blocked the road in front of us. I'm no zoologist, but I don't know any animal that could do that, trained or otherwise and certainly no human being could." Duke had also tried hard to rationalize what he'd seen, but there was no explaining the occurrence away. Still, he understood the desire. "I would have dismissed it as an overactive imagination if Sergeant Yazzie hadn't also seen it."

The sheriff sat back and nodded, as though he knew all that perfectly well. He looked toward the hallway, then faced Duke again. "I can't shake the feeling this creature is somehow interested in you and your recruitment activities. It's been popping up around Navajos who have enlisted or have an interest in the drive."

Duke considered that. "Are you sure that's the only connection? Gallup's a small town. Almost everyone's interested in the recruitment drive. Is there any chance there could be something else going on? Is there a geographic connection? Maybe this thing has a territory."

The sheriff shook his head. "You saw it on Route 66. I saw it north of town. Jerry Begay's folks are convinced a creature was involved in their son's death and I did find some hairs, just like Joe Nez did in his traps. That's south of town. If the creature has a territory, it's centered right square on Gallup, New Mexico."

"If it's connected to my recruiting mission here in town, the incidents should stop when we leave on Monday."

A creak sounded from the floor in the hallway. The sheriff glanced that way again, then lowered his voice. "What concerns me is what may happen between now and then."

Duke stood and put his hand on the sheriff's forearm. "Sir, trust me. I'll do everything I can to keep your daughter safe."

Davis nodded. "I know, son. And that's why I'm happy for you to take Cheryl out tonight."

Duke turned around and retrieved the flowers just as Cheryl came into the room. She wore a long skirt that hugged her hips and a jacket over a white blouse. It was her professional schoolteacher best. Duke wondered if she knew how wild that drove him. He recovered long enough to hand her the bouquet of flowers.

"They're wonderful." She smiled. "Let me put them in water before we go."

Davis took the flowers from his daughter. "That's a task even a man like me can handle. You can check my work when you get home." He turned to Duke. "I expect her back before too late," he said, as if they were a teenage couple.

Duke laughed with Cheryl, but he understood the sheriff's worry. He didn't expect a skinwalker to appear in the middle of town, but if it did, it could certainly ruin everyone's night. Off duty, Duke didn't wear a sidearm, but he'd made sure to stash one in the Willys's glove compartment. "We'll be back no later than twenty-one hundred hours, sir!" Duke spoke with exaggerated military precision hoping to maintain the light mood, even though he shared the sheriff's concerns.

Davis laughed and shook his hand. With that Duke led Cheryl out into the early evening dusk. "So, where do you plan to take me to tonight? Back to the Thunderbird Diner?"

"That was good, but tonight, I thought I'd treat us to something special. I thought we'd go to the Hotel El Rancho."

Cheryl's eyebrows shot up. "Really? That's where all the Hollywood types stay when they're in town making westerns. Why Lionel Barrymore and Ronald Reagan stayed there just a couple of years ago when they filmed The Bad Man."

"I figure if they attract all those Hollywood stars, the food in their restaurant can't be that bad. It'll certainly beat chow over at Fort Wingate." Duke opened the door for Cheryl.

After she climbed in, he went over to his side of the Willys and drove to where Route 66 passed through town, then turned into the El Rancho's parking lot. They walked into a two-story-high lobby with twin staircases. Between the staircases, a fire blazed in a stone hearth. Duke led Cheryl into the restaurant itself, where a waiter took them to a seat.

Only a few other people occupied the restaurant. In the years after the depression, few people had an income that supported going to a place this nice. Duke did have to restrain a gasp when he saw the prices on the menu, but then he looked up at Cheryl again and had no regrets about his decision to bring her here. They ordered steaks and Duke ordered a bottle of wine.

The waiter returned and poured a glass for each of them. Duke lifted a toast. "Here's to us."

Cheryl looked troubled at that. She ran her finger around the rim of her glass. "I have to admit, I've been wondering, is there really an 'us' or is this just a little fun before we return to our regular lives... before the war takes us separate directions?"

Duke set his glass down and reached out to take Cheryl's hand. "I wish I could predict what the coming years will bring for certain. What I have learned is that I want to get to know you better and if you're even half of the person who has infatuated me over the last few years, I would do anything to join you wherever you find yourself at the end of this war."

She looked up and met his gaze. "If you knew everything there is to know about me, I wonder if you would be as infatuated. I'm half Navajo and half white, but I never really fit into either world."

Duke laughed. "You can't tell anything about a person just by their appearance. Look at me. My ancestors came from Japan, but I know almost nothing about that culture."

"Would you like to know more about it?" Cheryl leaned forward, her gaze turning intense.

Duke shrugged. "At some point, sure. I might even like to go to Japan someday if our countries work out their differences."

Cheryl nodded. "When I was in college, I met some Navajos who helped me understand the part of my culture I'd been denied. They taught me some of the medicine ways and helped me find an inner strength I didn't know I possessed, but that strength scares me sometimes and I think I could use more training to control it."

Duke's brow furrowed. It seemed like Cheryl spoke some kind of code. "I don't understand what you're getting at."

She grinned, then took a sip of wine. "I didn't mean to unload old baggage on you. All I'm really saying is that I like you because I think we have more in common than someone might think at first glance. It's frustrating that the Marine Corps doesn't take women. I see the Corps has been good to you. Even so, I've been reading that the Army Signal Corps has been talking about recruiting telephone operators through the new Women's Army Auxiliary Corps they're setting up. If they do that, it seems they'd be interested in women radio operators. That might be a good way for me to advance my career."

"Really?" He smiled. "I thought your passion was numbers and equations."

"My passion..." She paused and lifted her glass. "My passion is logic and finding ways to improve people's lives. That's why I became a teacher. That's why I sought to understand the heritage I share with so many of my neighbors better. If I can find other ways to improve my lot in life or the lot of others, I'll take them."

Duke lifted his glass. "Here's to dreams. If that's your dream and I can help you achieve it, I will."

"I'll drink to that." Cheryl and Duke clinked their glasses and from that moment on, Duke had no thoughts about skinwalkers for the rest of the night.

Chapter Nine

Monday, March 2, 1942

Randall Yazzie and Duke Ogawa pulled into the parking lot at Gallup High School just as the sun rose on a cold, March morning. Clouds formed overhead. A storm had come in soon after their arrival in town. It seemed as though another one prepared to send them on their way. The gray clouds couldn't dampen Duke's spirits, though. His mind kept flitting back to Saturday night and the time he'd spent with Cheryl. Was the woman for him really his high school Math teacher from a few years ago? The rational part of his brain knew they needed more time before he would know for certain but time had run out for now. Still, his lips tingled, and the memory of her soft touch lingered.

Rand snapped his fingers in front of Duke's nose. "Looks like our new recruits are starting to arrive." They climbed from the Willys MB.

Two old trucks pulled up. In one case, a father and mother climbed out of the cab with their son. A whole family of kids hopped out of the bed of the other to see their brother off. Over the course of the next half hour, more vehicles arrived. One father and son arrived on horseback. Another family walked.

Rand allowed the recruits to stay with their families for as long as possible. They would be separated soon enough.

A green bus rolled down Route 66 toward the school and pulled into the parking lot. Several recruits already occupied seats. Duke sympathized with them. They had to have awoken a good two hours earlier to make their bus.

Rand and Duke told the recruits to say their good-byes and form up. Nineteen men got in line at the doors of the bus. They all looked so young to Duke. The diversity of the recruits also pleased him. There was the Ito boy and several white students. Two black kids stood in line along with eight Navajos. Duke regretted they hadn't done better, but they hadn't done bad. If some Navajo monster was trying to make them fail, they had beaten it.

As each recruit climbed on the bus, Rand checked their name off the list. Most seemed nervous. Some looked back at their families, as though wondering if they could still turn around and leave now that they had committed themselves. As the last person in line climbed onto the bus, Rand looked to Duke. "We're one short."

Just as he said that, a bright red 1932 Ford Roadster pulled into the parking lot with its top down. Miss Todachine sat behind the wheel and cast a contemptuous gaze around at all of the people. John Claw climbed out, tall and proud. He retrieved a bag from the backseat. The teacher and young man said no words, but Duke found himself wondering whether they shared a relation-ship like the one developing between him and Cheryl. It made his stomach do a flip-flop, but he shoved it aside as Claw approached.

"You're late, Mr. Claw," Rand observed.

"I had to wait for my ride," the Navajo said.

Rand ticked his name off the list and Claw climbed aboard the bus.

Families waved farewell and honked as the bus pulled out of the parking lot and back onto Route 66. Duke and Rand returned to the Willys MB and followed the bus to Fort Wingate. Duke looked around at the rolling terrain, jutting rocks, and occasional scrub brush. This place felt like home to him and he knew he'd be back.

He looked over to Rand. "So, what are your plans once this war is over?"

Rand shrugged. "I dunno. Probably go back home, but I haven't decided for certain. The beach around San Diego sure is nice. I could get used to living there if I can find a good job after we're discharged."

"Would you ever make a career of this?"

"The Corps?" Again, Randall shrugged. "Working stateside as a recruiter isn't bad, but it's not what I want to do for the rest of my life. I might consider applying for officer candidate school down the road."

"Good answer for a recruiter."

Rand chanced a quick glance at Duke. "What brought this on?"

Duke sighed. "Just contemplating the future. I'll probably come back here and work for my dad unless..." He allowed the words to trail off as he considered how big and unknown the future could actually be. Would his family be rounded up and locked away by the military? Would he be? What if the war presented Cheryl with new challenges and opportunities? Would she stay in Gallup? Would he follow?

His thoughts continued as they pulled up behind the bus, parked in front of Fort Wingate's administration complex. Duke and Rand hopped out of the Willys. A drill instructor on the bus shouted for the new recruits to get their butts out and stand at attention. Randall took his position in front of the men and administered the oath of enlistment. Duke noticed a photographer nearby recording the event. The photographer wore civilian clothes, which made Duke wonder whether he worked for one of the local newspapers.

After administering the oath, Rand stepped away from the podium. A few of the men began to relax. The drill sergeant from the bus shot forward and told them in no uncertain terms they had not been dismissed. One man looked at another. The drill sergeant stormed over. "Is he your sergeant?"

"No, sir?" came a nervous reply.

"Eyes forward!"

A few minutes later, Colonel Barr came out and addressed the assembled recruits. "I wanted to take this opportunity to say how proud I am that young men like you are willing to take a stand for your country."

Duke glanced at John Claw. Something like a sneer passed across the young man's face at those words. Or, did he just have an itchy nose? Maybe, but he was a new recruit. They usually just scratched instead of showing enough discipline to wait until an officer finished speaking. If he did scratch, there would be hell to pay with the drill sergeant.

When the colonel finished his address, he saluted the men. Rand, Duke, the drill sergeant, and the recruits snapped salutes. Barr nodded and returned to the building.

Two lance corporals joined the drill sergeant and marched the new recruits over to a tent, where they would receive their service record books and fill out paperwork. The sergeant and the corporals would yell at these new recruits and berate them, giving them the worst day of their life and making them grateful for the train's arrival later that night. Even so, Duke knew this would be the easiest day the new recruits would experience for a long time. He and Randall weren't drill sergeants. Their only job was to recruit the men and make sure they arrived in California.

The drill sergeant and lance corporals had taken the train into Grants where they met the bus and came in with the new recruits. Duke followed behind the recruits at a discrete distance. He heard the instructors yelling at them. He remembered his first weeks in the Corps. He'd never felt so humiliated in his life and yet he learned he could accomplish far greater things than he'd ever believed possible before.

"You need to go to the bathroom?" The shout came from within. "You will go when I damn well dismiss you."

There was silence. "The correct response is 'Aye aye, sir.'"

"Aye aye, sir," came the grudging response. Duke recognized the voice as John Claw.

"I didn't hear you!" the instructor shouted.

"Aye aye, sir!" John Claw's voice was sharper this time. Not just loud but angry. The Marines would take care of that.

Rand approached. "How are the maggots getting along?"

Duke shook his head. "Sounds like the drill sergeant is whipping them into shape."

Together the two walked over to the administration building to take care of some paperwork before their departure. They called their superior officer in California and reported their final number of recruits.

Their commander grunted. "Did you find any good candidates for the Navajo Language program?"

Duke flipped through the clipboard and checked his count. "It looks like we have a baker's dozen between our group from Gallup and the five Navajos from Farmington. They have potential to be good men once the drill sergeants get through with them."

"All right, this was a good first effort. I'll want to see you first thing on Monday morning."

"Yes, sir." Duke almost saluted the phone. Instead, he hung up. He and Rand left the administration building to pack up their gear for the trip. As they did, Duke spotted someone near the rail lines, peering into the window of one of the buildings. He realized it was John Claw. He tapped Rand on the shoulder and the two walked over to the recruit.

They just stood behind Claw and watched him. When he finally turned around, he startled, then recovered quickly and even had the temerity to smile. "Oh, Duke, I didn't see you."

"Recruit!" Duke didn't shout. He could never be a drill sergeant, but he could drill into a person with an icy stare. "You address me as 'sir.'"

Claw continued to smile, but he saluted. "Yes, sir."

Rand took a step toward him. "Where are you going, recruit?"

"I was looking for the latrine, sir."

"Latrine for the recruits is over there." Duke pointed to a building close to the tent where the drill instructors worked over the other new recruits.

"Yes, sir." Again, Claw snapped a salute.

"Do your business and get back where you belong," Duke ordered.

Claw nodded and strolled toward the latrine.

"Double time!" Randall called.

Claw picked up the pace and jogged.

Randall shook his head and looked at Duke. "Should we report him?"

Duke shook his head. "He'll get an ass chewing soon enough. But we should keep an eye on him until we head back to California."

Randall nodded and the two continued to their quarters to pack their belongings. Recalling his boot camp days, Duke stripped his bed and put the linens in the wash. He then returned with clean linens and made the bed so neat and tight he could bounce a quarter off it. Smiling to himself, he went to lunch with Randall.

Shortly after the sun set, the drill instructors marched a group of weary-looking and bedraggled recruits to the rail platform. Duke and Randall joined them. Duke glanced up and down the line of recruits. John Claw somehow didn't seem to be as tired as some of the others. His gaze wandered and Duke began to wonder if the new recruit had made any additional excursions during the day. What was Claw looking for? The buildings by the rail tracks didn't contain any major secrets. Any munitions ready for transportation would be boxed up in containers marked only with serial numbers. Somehow, Duke didn't think Claw was a spy, but he still seemed to be a troublemaker.

"Eyes forward, Craw!" called the old drill sergeant.

Duke chuckled. Drill sergeants often nicknamed the recruits. He supposed Claw had gotten up this guy's craw and the name stuck.

The Santa Fe locomotive chugged into the station and came to a stop. The recruiting sergeants boarded first. Duke took a seat by the window. He watched as the recruits began to board. Claw, near the back of the line, slipped back into the shadows.

Duke reached out and slapped Rand. "Claw's making a break for it."

The two leapt to their feet and went to the door. They pushed past the recruits. The drill instructors tried to ask what was happening. Duke knew they could help with the search, but he also knew if he took time to explain, Claw could get a big head start, especially if he'd already scouted out hiding places among the buildings—which must have been what he had been doing when Duke and Randall had approached him earlier.

Duke ran to the place where Claw had vanished from sight. From there, the recruit could have gone one of two directions between buildings. Randall took one path. Duke took the other.

The shadows closed in around Duke and he shivered. He doubted it was the cold that induced the reaction. He wished he had a flashlight as he peered in windows and tried doors. The buildings seemed secure. He pushed forward. At least the moon was high and bright, giving him some light. He drew his sidearm. He didn't want to shoot a recruit, but if Claw had made a run for it, he probably wouldn't go back peacefully. Duke figured he may have to persuade the man.

He continued between the warehouse buildings. When he finally reached the end, there was a clear shot to the fort's perimeter fence. A tall figure stood in the shadow of a tree beside a hole in the fence. "Claw!" he called.

The figure stepped out of the shadows into the moonlight. Its body was covered in hair and long ears lay back along its head. It dropped to all fours and sniffed the air. The skinwalker.

Duke aimed his sidearm. He didn't hesitate this time. He took aim and fired.

The creature leapt back into the shadow. Duke fired a second time. The creature bolted from its hiding place and ran toward Duke, who turned and ran back along the path he had followed. "Yazzie!" He called at the top of his lungs.

Rand appeared ahead. "What's wrong? I heard shots."

"Behind me!" Duke stopped beside Rand and whirled around.

The skinwalker had not followed him.

"I saw it. The creature was back," Duke panted.

The two ran back along the pathway between the buildings. Duke knew all too well they were hemmed in should the creature decide to charge them again. They reached the place where Duke had stood his ground but could see no sign of the skinwalker.

A pair of soldiers ran toward the hole in the perimeter fence. No doubt they were guards coming to investigate the gun fire.

Duke and Randall returned to the train. All the recruits had boarded. The drill sergeant stood beside a conductor, who tapped his foot and looked at his pocket watch. "Did you get Claw?" the sergeant asked.

Duke shook his head. "I don't know what happened to him."

The drill sergeant looked like he would grind his own teeth to powder. "Should we hold the train?"

The conductor shook his head. Duke held up his hand. "Just toss out my bag. It's past time I got to the bottom of what's going on around here."

"Toss mine out as well," Rand said.

The sergeant didn't argue. He just boarded the train and retrieved the bags.

Duke turned to his partner. "There's going to be hell to pay when we don't report as ordered on Wednesday morning."

"There's going to be even more hell to pay if we have to report that one of our promising recruits went AWOL on his first night." Rand shook his head. "There will probably be an inquiry about those shots you fired. I'm here to back you up."

Duke nodded. "Thanks. I appreciate that."

The conductor looked from Duke to the drill sergeant. "We're running late. We need to get going."

The drill sergeant boarded the train, followed by the conductor, who closed the door.

Duke looked at his watch. "Let's go make a phone call."

As they ran back to the barracks where they had been staying, the whistle blew, and the train pulled out of the station. Before they reached the door, two soldiers met them. "The captain of the watch wants to see you."

Duke and Rand exchanged glances. "Actually, we should coordinate with him," Rand said.

They followed the soldiers to their superior officer. He occupied a small office in the administration building. The captain asked about the gunshots and why they hadn't left on the train. Duke explained quickly about the missing recruit. He claimed ignorance of the gunshots and omitted any mention of the skinwalker.

"All right, we'll be on the lookout for your runner. If he's hiding on base, we'll find him," the captain said.

"May I use your phone, sir?"

The captain pushed the phone across the desk. Duke called Sheriff Davis and explained John Claw had disappeared. "I have his address on his recruitment forms," Duke said. "If Captain Foster is willing to let me use a vehicle, I can check his place, but I suspect he'll know we'll look for him there. The history teacher, Miss Todachine, brought him to the school this morning. If he left the base, she may be harboring him."

"I can check that out," the sheriff offered.

"Thank you," Duke said. He hung up the phone, wishing he could have warned the sheriff about the skinwalker. He had a feeling they hadn't seen the last of the creature that night.

Chapter Ten

Monday, March 2, 1942

Cheryl Davis arrived home later than normal. She had called and told her dad she had extra work at school, promising to get something to eat before coming home. Unable to keep her promise, her stomach growled as she dropped down in front of her ham radio set. Turning the frequency ever so slowly, her breath caught as she picked up familiar-sounding words.

She leaned forward and put her hands to the headset as she strained to listen. The accent and intonation reminded of her Navajo, but she couldn't make out specific words. She noted the frequency she was at. She needed a stronger signal. Operating under the assumption she'd hit a sideband frequency, she pulled out a piece of paper. A sideband alone wouldn't tell her the carrier frequency, but she could make some guesses. They tended to fall along predictable ratios. She made a few calculations based on the frequency.

She spun the dial down to her first guess and searched. Nothing. She spun down to her second. Still nothing. She chewed her lower lip, worried that the broadcaster may have simply finished their transmission. She spun down to her third guess. This time she hit the jackpot. The signal came through loud and clear. She still couldn't pick out any specific words, but she recognized the voice. It belonged to Miss Todachine. Cheryl wondered who she would be speaking to in Navajo.

A tap on Cheryl's shoulder startled her. She whirled around and ripped the headset from her head. Her dad stood behind her.

He wore his Montana hat and his sidearm. "I just got a call from Duke," he said.

She blinked several times in rapid succession. Her first thought was that she must not have heard the phone since she was listening so intently to the radio. Her second thought was that Duke should have left on the train to California. "Are you sure?" she asked. The look he gave her told her he was. She shook her head. "Why is he still in town?"

"One of the new recruits has gone AWOL. He thinks he may have made a run for Miss Todachine's house. I'm going over there to check it out."

Cheryl swallowed. "I was just about to let you know I picked up that strange transmission again, the one I thought was Navajo. I think I found the carrier frequency, or at least a stronger sideband." She waved her hands, collecting her thoughts. "I'm not sure if the person I heard was speaking Navajo, but I'm pretty sure I heard Miss Todachine's voice."

Her dad narrowed his gaze. "Now that's very interesting. Did you understand anything of what she said?"

"No. Without Mom or my college friends to practice with, I'm rusty. She spoke fast, and I couldn't really get what she said." She stood up.

"Your discovery may not be related and may not even be evidence of any wrongdoing." He nodded and turned for the door. "Still, I'm going to go over there and check this out."

Cheryl nodded. "Be careful."

Her dad grabbed his coat from the rack by the door and stepped out into the cold. Her mouth went dry as she watched him go. She worried about what he would find and what Duke would encounter. She wanted Duke on the train, a safe distance from Gallup, not trying to track down a deserter.

She noted the frequency where she'd picked up the signal, shut down the ham radio set, then went to her room and changed. She suspected Duke and her dad were up against more than they realized. She couldn't sit around at home and wait for them to tell her the aftermath. She stepped out into the cold.

Duke had memorized the directions the sheriff gave him, and he recited them as they drove out to the Claws' place. He looked around into the dark to the side of the car, half afraid he'd see the skinwalker chasing after them. He wasn't certain whether to be worried or relieved that it hadn't appeared again.

"So why exactly are we risking our careers chasing down this guy?" Rand asked. "We could have held the train and reported his disappearance to the military police. They could have dealt with this."

Duke had asked himself the same question several times already. "They're army. Do you think they're going to turn over every stone looking for a jarhead that went on the run?"

"So what?" Rand shrugged. "He ran and that pisses me off. No one deserts the Corps, but I also don't want to get booted out for his sake."

"This goes beyond the Corps. I'm afraid Cheryl and her dad may be in some danger," Duke admitted. "I don't know that for sure, but something in my gut tells me if they go looking for Claw, they're going to find the skinwalker."

"You know, so far this skinwalker has just been a trouble-maker. Has it actually killed anyone?"

Duke considered that. "What about Jerry Begay?"

Rand shook his head. "He froze to death. We don't know the skinwalker was involved. If it was, the only thing it did was lure him out into the snow. It's more like this thing gets you to do harm to yourself than it actually attacks and kills you."

As he scrambled to put the pieces together, Duke realized he nearly missed the next turn. He called out and Rand slammed on the brakes. They jolted forward, but then Rand turned the corner. Duke realized Rand had a point. The skinwalker didn't seem to hurt anyone. As that thought occurred to him, he re-membered something Sheriff Davis told him. "What about the mutilated cow?"

Rand blew a dismissive snort. "It's just a cow. It's not a person. Bad for the cow's owner, worse for the cow, but it's not the same as actually killing someone."

That response surprised Duke. He would have expected Rand to have more sympathy for a Navajo farmer and the plight of losing livestock.

They made one more turn, then followed a dirt road for about a mile until they came to a hogan with a fenced-in garden plot and sheep pens. Light shone from under the hogan's door and smoke rose from the chimney. Duke and Rand climbed from the Willys. Duke looked up to the sky and noted the full moon. He swallowed as he thought about watching The Wolf Man.

They walked up to the door and knocked.

An old Navajo with gray hair pulled back into a ponytail answered. "What may I do for you?" he asked.

Duke introduced himself and Rand. The old man shook their hands. "We're looking for John Claw," Duke said.

"I'm John's dad." The old man sighed and stepped outside, closing the door behind him. "Is he in trouble?"

"You might say that," Rand said. "He volunteered for the Marine Corps. We were about to board the train for California when he ran off."

The old man shook his head. He took a few steps away then turned around and faced Duke and Rand. "The Corps would do the boy good. I served in France during the last war. The boy does what he wants. I haven't seen him for over a year. We had a bad fight, and he hasn't been back."

Randall took a step toward the old man. "Do you have any idea where he might be?"

"You might ask that teacher…"

"Miss Todachine." Randall and Duke finished together.

"If anyone would know where he is, she would."

The two soldiers thanked the old man, then climbed back into the Willys and hurried toward Gallup.

Sheriff Davis stepped out of his patrol car and strode up Miss Todachine's walk. He took a moment and listened. He could make out voices from within. He pounded on the door. When no answer came, he listened again. This time he only heard silence. He pounded one more time. "This is Sheriff Davis. I'd like to talk to you."

A moment later, Miss Todachine appeared at the door. She wore a bathrobe and the sheriff's first impression was that he had awoken her. Then he realized she wore outdoor shoes and the long sleeves that protruded below the robe's cuffs looked more like day-wear than pajamas. "What can I do for you, Sheriff."

"I'm looking for one of your associates, Mr. John Claw," the sheriff declared. "He signed up for military service, then deserted this evening. Do you know his whereabouts?"

She gave the sheriff an exaggerated yawn, then looked at the watch on her wrist. "Sheriff, it's late. I don't know where Mr. Claw is."

As she spoke the words, a Willys MB pulled up in front of the house. Duke and Rand clambered out and strode up to the door.

"Any luck at the Claw place?" the sheriff asked.

Duke shook his head. "I spoke to his father. He hasn't seen John in over a year."

The sheriff turned to the teacher. "Would it be okay if we came in and looked around?"

Miss Todachine folded her arms and narrowed her gaze. "Do you have a warrant?"

Before the sheriff could answer, Duke interjected. "You dropped Mr. Claw off at the high school this morning. There's good reason to believe you..." Duke seemed to struggle to find the right words.. "There's good reason to believe you have a relationship with him."

"He's a former student and he doesn't have a car. He asked me to bring him to the high school." She looked at each man in turn. "Now, unless you have a warrant, I suggest you get off my property."

The sheriff turned toward Duke. "She's right. Let's go over to the sheriff's office. I'll put in a call to Judge Stone. He'll write out a warrant tonight." He turned back to Miss Todachine. "Don't get too comfortable, we'll be back soon."

She stepped back inside and had nearly pushed the door closed when a crash and a scream came from within.

"Yee naaldlooshii!"

Rand looked at Duke and translated. "Skinwalker!"

The sheriff pushed past Miss Todachine. Just as he entered the house, John Claw came running in from a back room, his face pale. "Frankie, Frankie!" He spoke rapid Navajo.

Rand again translated. "He says he was waiting out in the back yard when the skinwalker arrived."

The sheriff was torn. They'd found their man. They could take him into custody and call it a night, but what did he mean about the skinwalker being out back? Wasn't Miss Todachine or this John Claw guy the skinwalker? She spoke Navajo back at Claw. The young man fought to compose himself. His terror was no ruse. He'd seen something.

The sheriff made a decision. He pulled a set of handcuffs from his belt and slapped one side on Claw. He grabbed Miss Todachine's wrist and cuffed her hand. "What the hell are you doing?"

Somehow the sheriff wasn't shocked by her unladylike language. He pointed to Claw. "You are a deserter." He pointed to Todachine. "You have been harboring a fugitive from justice. I think you both have questions to answer, but I have another question to answer first." He turned to Randall and Duke. "Watch them 'til I get back."

They looked as though they wanted to protest, but understood they couldn't leave the two on their own. The sheriff ran into the back room, which proved to be a kitchen. At the far end, a door led out into the back yard. It had been left open and a cold wind blew in. He ran to the door and peered out into the night. At first, he didn't see anything, despite the bright moonlight. Then he saw a pair of eyes from near a tree.

The sheriff drew his revolver and stepped out into the cold. Was the skinwalker a person in a suit, or was it an animal? He was determined to find out. "You there! Come out with your hands up."

A growl sounded from behind the tree.

The sheriff aimed the revolver at the ground in front of the creature. His hand trembled, whether from fear or the cold, he didn't know. He fired.

The creature backed off and vanished into the shadows. The sheriff followed. It scrambled over the back fence. The sheriff holstered his revolver and jumped. He pulled himself up just in time to see a flash of light. He dropped back to the ground, blinking back an afterimage. He looked through the fence's slats. He didn't see the soap-bubble-like glow he had before, but neither did he see the skinwalker. It appeared the creature had vanished. The afterimage bothered him, and he hoped it was more imagination than reality.

He ran back to the house and into the living room where John Claw and Frances Todachine waited, looking uncomfortable as the two Marine sergeants watched over them.

"What did you see?" Duke asked.

"I saw the creature, but it's gone now."

"But I thought..." Duke looked from Miss Todachine and Claw to the sheriff. He didn't speak his thoughts aloud.

The sheriff stepped closer to the apprehended pair. "Do you two want to tell me what's going on?"

"We don't have to tell you anything," Todachine spat the words.

"You do have that right." The sheriff nodded slowly. "But right now, my suspicion is that you're spying."

Todachine's eyes widened and her mouth fell open. She seemed shocked. "Why in the world would you think that?"

"I caught Mr. Claw wandering around Fort Wingate," Duke said. "Earlier today, he'd gone AWOL from the training instructors and I found him poking around where he shouldn't."

"You're right," Claw said. "I never intended to go with you, but I wasn't spying... exactly." He looked toward the teacher. "She wanted me to learn how the Marine Corps treated Indians so we could tell others. We wanted to know why you were so interested in recruiting Navajos. We're nothing more than cannon fodder for white soldiers." He cast a pointed gaze at Rand. "Isn't that right, brother?"

Rand ignored him.

The sheriff looked at the teacher. "My daughter heard you on the radio tonight. She thought you were speaking Navajo. Was it some kind of code? Were you selling secrets?"

Duke and Randall looked at each other. The sheriff didn't quite understand the perplexed look they shared, but that didn't really matter.

"She heard?" Miss Todachine blew out a snort. "I was speaking to our O'Odham brothers in Arizona, warning them about the Marine recruiters. I see your plot, using Indians, black people, Mexicans..." She cast a pointed gaze at Duke. "...Japanese people to catch bullets so you can win victories against your enemies. What's more, you'll finally be rid of us. Rid of the thorns in your sides."

"I am in the Corps to serve my homeland," Randall said.

The sheriff cleared his throat. "You don't have to explain yourself to her." He looked from Claw to Todachine. "However, you two will have to explain yourselves to a judge." He looked up to the Marine sergeants. "Can I impose on you two to help me get these two over to the sheriff's station?"

"We'd be glad to help," Duke said.

They began to lead the two suspects outside to the car.

"Did you learn anything about the skinwalker?" Duke asked.

The sheriff shook his head. He didn't want to discuss the afterimage that still haunted him. The one he knew he'd have to forget for his sanity. He closed his eyes for a moment and saw Cheryl's face staring back at him.

Epilogue

Monday, April 13, 1942

Sheriff Davis received a phone call from the mayor. "The town council meeting is in half an hour. I know you wanted to say some words."

"I'll be there." Davis hung up and shoved some papers into a briefcase and walked out to the Mercury Eight. Last week, the mayor had received a telegram from Washington. They were to round up all citizens of Japanese descent and remand them to Colonel Barr at Fort Wingate, where he would take custody and send them to an internment camp.

The wind ripped through Gallup, blowing dust and debris through the streets. It looked a little like a Hollywood western town ready for a showdown. Davis felt as lonely as any Hollywood lawman. After arresting Frances Todachine and John Claw, he came home to find a hastily scrawled note. Cheryl had packed her bags and left. She intended to catch the next bus out of town. She signed off saying, "I'm sorry for all the trouble I caused."

The day the mayor received the telegram from Washington, Davis had received a longer letter from his daughter. She told him she'd gone to Des Moines, Iowa to join up with the new Women's Auxiliary Army Corps. She hoped this would provide a path to entering the Army Signal Corps where she could put her radio skills to use. She closed the letter with an odd phrase. "I have discovered how to unleash great power. Now I need to bring that power to heel."

Had his daughter really been the skinwalker creature he'd seen? Cheryl loved her Navajo heritage but she lost most of her ties to the culture when her mother died. Davis had been glad when his daughter reported making Navajo friends in college. Had they helped her learn ancient, forbidden medicine?

Davis pulled up at City Hall. He climbed the steps and entered the meeting chamber just as the mayor banged the gavel and called the meeting to order.

The councilors started the meeting and conducted routine business. It took half an hour to get to the meeting's primary focus. The mayor read the letter he had received from Washington. It claimed the action against Japanese-Americans was being taken in the interest of national security. "Before we vote, I believe Sheriff Davis had a few words."

The sheriff stood and cleared his throat. "Yes, sir. I just wanted to tell you about a young man I recently had the pleasure of getting to know, Duke Ogawa. As many of you are aware, he recently came to town to recruit young men for the war effort. During that time, we discovered a small group of people were attempting to interfere with that effort."

Frances Todachine and John Claw still sat in jail, awaiting trial. They wanted to keep young men from throwing away their lives, but was that a crime? Davis would have to let a judge decide.

"When Mr. Claw deserted Fort Wingate, Mr. Ogawa took appropriate action and contacted me. He helped me apprehend these people who would interfere with the war effort. Mr. Ogawa showed that despite his heritage, he was a true American patriot who will stand up for his country. I have known his parents, Mr. and Mrs. Ken Ogawa for many years..."

He went into detail about the Ogawa's and their journey from Los Angeles to Gallup. He then spoke about the Ito's and other Japanese families around town.

"Thank you for your testimony," the mayor said. He asked if anyone else had comments. Several people from around town stood and spoke on behalf of their friends and neighbors. That's what the sheriff loved most about Gallup and about New Mexico. People cared about each other. It didn't matter much where their ancestors came from, it mattered what actions they took.

If Cheryl had been the skinwalker, he could only guess the reasons she had taken the actions she did. She seemed sorry about Jerry Begay's death. He suspected she'd hoped to scare him a little, encourage him to stay home, at least until he finished high school. She surely didn't intend for him to die. He thought back to the other encounters. Cheryl must have been watching out for Duke and him. If he'd invited her to accompany him to Standing Rock, the skinwalker probably would never have appeared.

People in the audience finished their comments. The town council held a vote.

The mayor nodded at the results. "The nays have it. We are agreed there is no creditable threat from those people in this town with Japanese ancestry. We will not comply with the executive order from Washington."

No round of applause. Not much reaction at all aside from a few people murmuring to themselves and a few smiles. All in all, Davis sensed contentment and relief.

He'd done what he could for Duke's family. He would go home and write a letter to Cheryl. All he could do was encourage her in her new path. He hoped that path would help her find a way to control the "great power" she'd found. If not, he knew any who stood in her way would face serious consequences.

ABOUT THE AUTHOR

David Lee Summers is the author of a dozen novels and numerous short stories and poems. His most recent novels are the space pirate adventure, Firebrandt's Legacy, and a horror novel set an astronomical observatory, The Astronomer's Crypt. His short stories have appeared in such magazines and anthologies as Cemetery Dance, Realms of Fantasy, Straight Outta Tombstone, After Punk, and Gaslight and Grimm. He's one of the editors of Maximum Velocity: The Best of the Full-Throttle Space Tales from WordFire Press. He's been nominated for the Science Fiction Poetry Association's Rhysling and Dwarf Stars Awards. When he's not writing, David operates telescopes at Kitt Peak National Observatory. He's also been known to drive lonely desert roads, watching for cryptids. Find David on the web at http://www.davidleesummers.com.

artist's rendition of a Skinwalker

SKINWALKERS

(Also called *Yee naaldlooshii*, which translates into "with it, he goes on all fours" in the language of the Diné — or Navajo .)

ORIGINS: Versions of human shapshifters exist around the world. In North America, there are among the native tribes multiple versions of what are called skinwalkers. These are witches that have joined the secret society of skinwalkers by violating cultural and sacred taboos, performing a ritual dance meant to curse rather than heal to gain power and magic for selfish ends.

The highest rank of these witches complete an act such as cannibalism, incest, or killing a close blood relative to attain their power.

DESCRIPTION: Skinwalkers have the ability to become any animal they chose by donning the creature's pelt, though they can change without doing so. Because of this, the Navajo have a cultural taboo against wear furs, particularly those of predators.

Often skinwalkers are said to appear as coyotes, crows, wolves, or other predators, but they can chose the form to suit their current needs. They can even appearing as another human being by stealing the face of the person. Their ability to transform can also extend to their voice, allowing them to lure victims with what sounds like a baby crying or a loved one's voice.

Whatever form they take on, one can recognize them in their tranformed state by their supernatural spead, their malformed shape, and their glowing animal eyes. To meet that unnatural gaze is to give the witch power over you.

It is also said that to say the word skinwalker is to draw their attention to you, so they are not talked about openly or among non-native individuals.

HISTORY: Due to the cultural taboo against speaking of this creature, there are not a lot of specific accounts, beyond the events at Sherman — or Skinwalker — Ranch, in Ballad, Utah, but there have been many accounts of coyotes and other animals pacing cars at great speeds on secluded roadways, and behaving in other unnatural ways.

About the Artist

Although Jason Whitley has worn many creative hats, he is at heart a traditional illustrator and painter. With author James Chambers, Jason collaborates and illustrates the sometimes-prose, sometimes graphic novel, The Midnight Hour, which is being collected into one volume by eSpec Books. His and Scott Eckelaert's newspaper comic strip, Sea Urchins, has been collected into four volumes. Along with eSpec Books' Systema Paradoxa series, Jason is working on a crime noir graphic novel. His portrait of Charlotte Hawkins Brown is on display in the Charlotte Hawkins Brown Museum.

CAPTURE THE CRYPTIDS!

Cryptid Crate is a monthly subscription box filled with various cryptozoology and paranormal themed items to wear, display and collect. Expect a carefully curated box filled with creeptastic pieces from indie makers and artisans pertaining to bigfoot, sasquatch, UFOs, ghosts, and other cryptid and mysterious creatures (apparel, decor, media, etc).

http://CryptidCrate.com